WHAT MAKES GRANDPA TICK?

By: Marshall H. Ervin

WHAT MAKES GRANDPA TICK?

Copyright © 1997
First Printing 1997

Published By

BOOKS OF JOY
509 W. Madison • Rushville, IL 62681
1-217-322-6930

Library of Congress Card Catalog Number: 97-90801
ISBN: 1-57502-557-4

Printed in the USA by

MORRIS PUBLISHING

3212 East Highway 30 • Kearney, NE 68847 • 1-800-650-7888

DEDICATION

This book is dedicated to Robbie,
our four children,
nine Grandchildren,
and nine great-Grandchildren.

ACKNOWLEDGMENTS

This book is what it is today because of two special people, and I would like to thank them for everything they've done.

To Robbie, my wife and best friend. Thanks for your patience and understanding during the many hours I spent in front of a computer screen.

To Lorrie Farrington, my editor. Thanks for your wisdom, skills, and your kindness. Your encouragement and suggestions have made it possible for me to start over and keeping working in times of discouragement.

To Jane Boyd, Rose Rebman Mrs. Paul Morris, and Cheryl Baker for help in the early stages of this book.

To Lester & Joan Robertson for the cover photography and Diane Edwards for assistance with the cover design and other materials.

To Scott Henley, my pastor, for your prayers and support.

FOREWORD

With the approach of the year 2000, Americans—always obsessed with milestones—are taking stock as never before, but with greater difficulty. Our renewed search for a "usable past," for patterns from the last millennium that might apply to the next, is complicated by factors we can barely comprehend, let alone control.

For one thing, the rate of change is more rapid now than at any time in human history, and its impact is more profound. For another, though the American population is aging, the generation gap is also widening. Thus today's young find it harder to access the experience and advice of their elders.

It is in this context that I find Marshall Ervin's reminiscences and reflections so refreshing. During a successful career as a Methodist minister in the Midwest, he regularly faced the challenge of translating values into contemporary terms and helping churchgoers reconcile the eternal with the transient. Now that retirement offers him a chance for relief from that professional pressure, however, Ervin refuses to embrace oblivion. Instead, at age 81, he has reinvented himself as an author in search of a new audience.

Ervin's story is inspiring not only for what it tells us but also in how it came to be told. He introduced himself to me in November of 1996 at a workshop for aspiring writers on the campus of the University of Illinois at Springfield, where I teach English. He had enrolled because he was working on a manuscript prompted by a grand-daughter who wanted to know what made him tick. Writers' workshops usually attract the dilettantish as well as the dedicated, and Ervin was easily the oldest participant in this one, but I was struck by his confidence and commitment. Six months later, when I was asked to contribute this foreword to the completed project, I was pleased, but not surprised, that he had finished his book.

I felt doubly rewarded as I lingered over his recollections and ruminations, the residue of a rich and thoughtful life captured in a voice at once familiar and engaging. Whether he is discussing birth or death, sickness or health, solitude or union, Ervin combines the warmth and wisdom of a tribal elder with the gentle humor and seasoned humanity of a small-town sage. Whatever your age— grandparent or grandchild—he will help you consider what matters in the midst of uncertainty, what lasts in the face of change. His brand of common sense is increasingly uncommon, and therefore all the more welcome, in our time.

Judith Everson
June 1997
Springfield, Illinois

Dr. Judith L. Everson is the Professor and Chair of the English Program of School of Liberal Arts and Sciences University of Illinois at Springfield. Dr. Everson is also the President of the James Jones Literary Society.

TABLE OF CONTENTS

PROLOGUE

A perplexed and admiring Granddaughter once said, "Grandpa, you are really a character! I wonder what makes you tick?" Something clicked in Grandpa's mind, and he had the title for this book. Grandpa says, "Thanks to my Granddaughter."

This is a story that is told by Grandpa! It is his wish that this book will cause you to smile and laugh often, and that you will shed a few tears as well. Grandpa has a firm conviction that persons ought to laugh more! The focus of the story is on the family. Grandpa hopes you will become more aware of how God's presence works in the daily lives of ordinary folks, to forgive their sins, heal their hurts, and to make them whole.

Grandpa makes no attempt to be scientifically or historically accurate. It is not a theological treatise. It is told in the language of common folk. Biblical references are not copied from any translation or version, but are Grandpa's free translations from memory. It is simply a tale that is told and is a mixture of fact and fiction.

Grandpa says, 'I loved every minute of spinning this yarn."

Pull up your most comfortable chair, relax, and enjoy Grandpa's tale!

CHAPTER 1
CREATIVE PROCESS

Once upon a time Grandpa took the first step of an incredible journey...

In the beginning God...

Grandpa says, "You can't get much further back than the beginning. Nothing comes out right in life unless you begin with God. Without God there is no meaning or purpose. "

Grandpa thinks God was very clever when he stood on the edge of newness, confronted by void and darkness, and in his mind conceived a spectacular heaven and earth. He spoke a creative word and it was. He flung the stars, moon, sun, and the planets into their orbits. WOW! What a big bang! It has been reverberating down through the corridors of time ever since (Perhaps this is where Carl Sagan and his gang got on board).

Once again God stood on the edge of newness and imagined a man and made him in his own image to enjoy all these wonders with him.

Grandpa says, "Let's take a look at how it all happened when God conceived this incredible process."

God took a little mud, looked it over carefully, and then shaped it to look like himself. He breathed on the mud, low and behold, there was Adam in his own image, a living soul.

God stepped back, took a good look, and declared, "it's not too bad! In fact, it is good."

1

God started laughing, and it seemed his sides would split. (Grandpa believes in a God who laughs and is happy).

God said, "Adam you are good, but you are good for nothing! If you are going to help me with my plan, you can't do it alone, you need someone to help you." (A man never amounts to much by himself).

God reached over and touched Adam's chest and flipped out a rib. He took a little more mud. He shaped it up and breathed on the mud and there was Eve! Was she ever alive! She had long slender legs, shapely breasts, and a lovely face. Her eyes were a deep brown that immediately got Adam's attention and left him breathless. Her lovely auburn hair was her crowning glory and fell in waves over her shoulders.

Adam was the first man to ever sing the doxology. He fell on his knees in awe and wonder and sang, "Praise God from whom all blessings flow."

God said, "You two are going to enjoy helping me with my plan to recreate life and populate the earth." They both gladly agreed to cooperate.

Grandpa says, "That is cranking up an amazing process very quickly." Grandpa offers his apologies to Carl Sagan and his "Big Bang" theory. Sagan just does not go far enough back. The creative process is much easier to believe, much more interesting, and a lot more fun!

Scientists seek truth about the "nuts and bolts," the physical and mechanical nature of the universe. The biblical writers seek truth about the ultimate questions of life:

THE WHO?

WHY?

MEANING?

PURPOSE OF LIFE?

Grandpa says, "Struggling with these questions is absolutely essential to a good life."

Grandpa says, "There is no argument between biblical truth and scientific truth. Truth is truth, regardless of the source. Science and biblical truth are friends that need each other to remind us that no one has all the answers, and that the truth we hold is partial. We see through a glass darkly." It is when either science or religion make false claims that we get into trouble. We are not God!

Grandpa says, "One thing for sure, the biblical writer was correct when he wrote, 'In the beginning God...'" That is truth whether it was 5000 B.C. or a billion years, or many aeons ago. Life is meaningless without God. You cannot get any further back than the "beginning." Grandpa says, "If you do not get back to God, you are not far enough into the past, and the future will have no meaning."

The creative process never runs out of steam, and it is easy to understand why. All God needs is a little cooperation from a man and a woman. He gave them plenty of motivation for getting the job done.

In 1916 God said, "It is time for Grandpa! Let's see what can he do?" It happened in the family home in Cape Girardeau, in Southeast Missouri, on the banks of the mighty Mississippi River. God wound the clock and Grandpa started ticking.

God smiles on a young mother giving birth to her son. The mother smiles at her husband and says, "God has given us another son." They had lost their first son at three years of age, and a daughter at the same age. Another daughter was born with a physical handicap. They were filled with grief, but now found hope and joy in this newborn son.

Grandpa heard this story many times as a youngster, and he felt the warmth of God's smile as he took the first step of his incredible journey. He was aware that God is good.

Grandma made her grand entrance in 1919 at the family home in rural Crittenden County, Kentucky, not far from the banks of the Ohio River. God smiles on her mother and father late in life and gave them a beautiful baby girl with large brown eyes.

It was just as inevitable that Grandma and Grandpa should meet as that the Ohio and Mississippi Rivers should meet a few miles south of their homes

Grandpa met Grandma in a delicatessen where college and high school kids gathered to drink cokes and dance.

The first time he looked into her dark brown eyes Grandpa said. "This is the girl I have been dreaming of all my life." Sparks began to fly, and their body chemistry went to work immediately. Grandpa was never the same after that moment.

Grandpa was a big band enthusiast and after graduation from high school he organized a dance band. During the time he was dating Grandma, he was broadcasting daily from a radio station K.F.V.S. while playing in the Rainbow Room of the Idanha Hotel, located at Broadway and Fountain, in downtown Cape Girardeau. He sang love songs to Grandma via the air waves. Each evening he would croon love songs such as "Star Dust," "1 Love You." and "1 Only Have Eyes for You." Grandma would always be listening. This fanned the flames of romance and kept the relationship growing more intimate. Grandpa was an incurable romantic and still is at 80 years of age.

Two kids became one on March 22, 1936. Grandma and Grandpa stood before a Methodist clergyman with a wooden leg, at the altar of the Methodist Church in Corning, Arkansas, and said, "I Do!"

Grandpa says, "1 am not sure marriages are made in heaven, but I am certain that God is actively at work in marriages that are made here on earth."

Grandpa thinks God smiled and said. "They are both young, don't have much sense, and no money. However, they do have guts, love each other, are willing to work and learn. If they will let me help them, I think they will make it." Time has proved God was right over the past 60 years plus.

Grandpa remembers his father saying, "She was born in Old Kentucky. Take her boy, you're mighty lucky." Grandpa did exactly what his father told him to do (At least in this instance). Grandpa rejoices over his father's advice and is exceedingly glad he picked Grandma.

God smiled and said, "I think you two better get busy helping me with my creative plans before you get in trouble. Grandpa and Grandma thought it was a good idea. They rolled up their sleeves and went to work. Did they ever have fun! (Also a few problems). They produced four children, nine grandchildren, eight great grandchildren, and there are more on the way. That is what you call cooperation. At eighty, Grandpa still thinks when God gives you a job, the best thing to do is take the first step as quickly as possible. You must give it your best shot and "hang in there" until the job is done.

Grandpa thought, "Boy, this is a great way to help God." Grandpa had a lot to learn.

Grandpa and Grandma were elated when Grandma got pregnant for the first time. She was very trim, weighing only 105 pounds. Things soon began to change, and she put on some weight. Grandma loved watermelon and craved it during her pregnancy. She had a good friend who lived next door who also was pregnant and loved watermelon. They bought melons and hid them under the beds to keep their husbands from knowing how many they were eating. It was a great secret that could not be hidden. Grandpa thought that their first child would look like a watermelon. Grandpa was learning many things about Grandma and about life in general. What Grandpa loved to do was place his hands on Grandma's stomach and feel the baby kick. It was the thrill of a life time.

It was a high and holy moment when the first son was born on September 16, 1937. The nurse at Southeast Missouri Hospital placed the little guy in Grandpa's arms. Grandpa's heart was filled with pride and joy. The baby's face was red, and he had black hair that came down so far on his forehead that the nurses nicknamed him "Chief Wahoo?" Grandpa and Grandma had taken a few steps in God's eternal plan to replenish the earth! Life is truly good!

To say the least, Grandpa was excited! He rushed out of the hospital and went to baby's clothing store where he purchased a pair of little bib overalls. He didn't know much about sizes and overestimated the size of his son. The kid was not able to wear them until he was two years old. Grandpa went everywhere and called everyone he knew proclaiming his good news. "We have a new son!" No other experience in life is comparable to the birth of your first child. Grandpa says, "Surely God alone could think up this amazing process." It is an awesome process if you have the eyes to see.

When they brought the new baby home Grandpa and Grandma soon learned that being a parent is not all fun. There is a lot of hard work involved in being a good father and mother. "Guts" and "grace" are necessary ingredients. It takes a lot of guts and all the grace God can give you to fulfill the daily role of a parent (grandpa loves the word "guts," even the computer lights up when you use it).

Babies wet and mess in their pants! (I do mean mess). At the time when Grandma and Grandpa's first child was born, diapers had to be washed and fastened with safety pins. (Pampers were not yet made). Babies cry at night and wake you up at the most inconvenient hours! A full night's sleep is rare indeed. Grandma usually jumped up first when the baby cried! When she was exhausted, Grandpa would crawl out of bed and take his turn. God laughed and said, "He seems to be reluctant, but he is learning."

Grandpa says, "Patience has its rewards, but it is a hard virtue to come by when a baby is crying at night. Only the tough survive."

The rocking chair is a must! It is an absolute necessity with your first baby. Grandma and Grandpa inherited a one-sided rocker, with one rocker worn more than the other. Grandpa would croon or hum a lullaby as he rocked the baby, and the old chair would walk across the room from one side to the other. He would then move back and start all over, repeating this until the baby would fall asleep. Grandpa felt a sense of satisfaction, and forever after associated what little patience he has acquired with the rocking chair. It is still his favorite chair.

A feeding formula for babies is a real challenge! The baby did well with breast feeding for a short period of time. The doctor decided the baby needed a formula. The first one grandma and grandpa tried made the baby constipated. There were more sleepless nights, with a diaper over the shoulder to burp the little guy at midnight, 2 a.m. and 4 a.m. and sometimes he would wake up in between. The burps often turned into "urps" that ran down the neck and back (a real shock at 2 a.m.). Grandpa got so tired that he would fall back into bed, and in spite of the smell he would soon be fast asleep. When the doctor suggested a new formula adding lactic acid, the same routine began again. The baby finally gave up and began to digest the formula. He must have realized that formulas would just keep coming until he did. When things seemed to level off, Grandpa and Grandma gave a sigh of relief and rejoiced over having lived through it. They were learning that it is things like these that are the realities of being parents. (A real university of life).

Grandpa would be the first to admit that he was far from being a perfect father, but he was learning. He would get aggravated at the baby and Grandma as well. It is hard to be a loving father in the middle of the night when your baby is crying and won't go to sleep. Grandma and Grandpa "hung in there," learning and persevering.

Grandpa says, "After 60 years of marriage, we are still learning and persevering. It is a life long process, requiring much hard work and God's constant help."

Babies attract all kinds of visitors! Some of the visitors would try the patience of Job (neither Grandpa or Grandma had that kind of patience). The baby has just gone to sleep, and the doorbell rings (It will do it every time). In comes Louise Lipp to see the baby. Grandma tiptoes into the nursery with the visitor following and talking as fast and as loud as possible. It is quite evident her first priority is to wake the baby (Grandma places her finger on her lips to signify the need for quiet). It is all to no avail and the baby lets out a loud scream and begins bawling. Louise reaches into the cradle and pinches the baby's cheek saying, "Isn't he cute! Can I hold him?" As she takes him in her arms, he continues to bawl louder and holds his breath! Finally she can stand it no longer, hands him to Grandma and says, "I must run. I just came for a few minutes." Mission accomplished, she hurries out. Grandma gives a sigh of relief and gets busy putting the baby back to sleep.

Grandpa says, "Lipp is a very appropriate name for Louise."

Grandma's friend, Justine Wright, knocked gently on the door. When Grandma opens the door, Justine quietly asks, "Is it convenient for me to visit the new baby?" She continues, "If it is not the right time I can come back at another time. I know from experience it is very trying to have someone come in when the baby is sleeping." She and Grandma slip quietly into the room and watch as the baby sleeps like a lamb. When they slip back into the living room she says, "He is really a fine baby. If you ever need me, I will be glad to sit with him while you run an errand or get a little rest." She quietly excuses herself and is gone. What an inspiration for two young parents. Grandpa could not help but exclaim, "Justine is so right! Wright is the right name for her."

Grandpa says, "I think God planned the frustrations and hardships related to the birth and the care of our child in order that a little character might rub off on Grandma and me." Grandpa continues, "Time has proved me right." God is at the beginning, at the end, and every place in between! Grandpa says, "We are challenged to recognize him at work in all our experiences in every day life."

Grandpa says, "BABIES ARE LIKE SUNSHINE, THEY JUST KEEP COMING!"

Something new and different was in store when Grandma became pregnant two years later. The doctor suggested that Grandma remain at home for the birth of their second baby. He turned to Grandpa and said, "Every young father ought to be present and witness the birth of one of his babies." (This was long before Lamaze classes). Grandpa was in a state of shock. He had not expected such a suggestion. To be real honest, it scared him to death. However, he reluctantly agreed to the doctor's suggestion. (Doctors know best).

Grandma escaped the craving for watermelon during this pregnancy. As the date drew near for delivery, a retired registered nurse, who lived next door, offered to help take care of Grandma until the doctor would arrive and to assist him during the delivery. This nurse had assisted the doctor on numerous occasions. This relieved Grandpa's anxiety, knowing that someone would be available until the doctor would arrive.

Grandpa says, "Grandma was always more beautiful when she was pregnant." He loved her with a passion and worried about her health during the nine month period. The doctor assured him that everything was going along just fine, and said, "Anyone who has babies as easy as Grandma ought to have a dozen." Grandpa very carefully told the doctor that he thought that was carrying things too far. This was one time that Grandma agreed fully with Grandpa.

As the time drew near for the date of delivery, Grandpa and Grandma were looking forward with great expectations. About 1 a.m. February 3rd, Grandma awakened Grandpa and informed him that she was having some pains. She said, "I think the time is here." He got excited and paced the floor trying to think what to do. Grandma came to his rescue and reminded Grandpa of the nurse next door. He hurriedly put on his shirt and pants, grabbed a jacket, and rushed out the door in his bare feet, stepping into six inches of newly fallen snow. He had forgotten to put on his socks and shoes. He dared not take time to go back and get them, so he waded next door and knocked. When the door opened, he shouted, "She is having pains, comes quickly." The neighbor glanced at Grandpa's bare feet and started laughing. She assured Grandpa everything was going to be "ok" and sought to calm him down. She telephoned the doctor, put on her coat and galoshes, and opened the door (Grandpa following in his bare feet). When they got into the house, the nurse began to time the intervals between contractions. She looked at Grandpa and said, "it is not going to be long, I sure hope the doctor gets here in time." She told Grandpa to get busy and heat some water. She gave him several things to do in order to keep him busy and out of trouble.

As the contractions became closer, the nurse expressed concern. She said, "If that doctor doesn't get here soon, you and I will have to deliver the baby." The nurse gave Grandpa some pointed instructions and told Grandma to squeeze her legs together and maybe the baby would not come before the doctor arrived. Grandpa felt like he was going to faint but he "hung in there" and kept working. Grandma was in excruciating pain, and large drops of sweat rolled off her face. Grandpa rubbed her face with a cold wet cloth and held her hand. He did his best to comfort her. There was a soft knock on the door, and the doctor walked hurriedly through the door. The nurse shouted, "Doctor hurry up, this baby is being born." The doctor quickly washed his hands in hot water and was by the nurse's side. In what seemed like only a few moments, he looked up at Grandpa saying, "Young man you have a fine son!" As he lifted the baby up, it began to cry, and so did Grandpa and Grandma. Grandpa kissed Grandma and gently patted her hand. In a few moments, the doctor said, "Grandma is doing just fine and so is the baby." It was a time of rejoicing.

The birth of their second baby was again a very sacred and growing experience in both Grandpa and Grandma's lives. It was a lesson in the experience of pain and joy intermingled. Grandpa spent many hours thinking and wondering why God allowed women to suffer so much pain in such a joyous experience as childbirth. Grandpa says, "After 80 years, I still do not understand fully the meaning of suffering; however, I am convinced it is a builder of character and a learning experience we all need." Grandpa is grateful for the mental and emotional anguish he shared with Grandma during the birth of their second child. He thinks the doctor was right when he said, "Every young man should be at the bedside when his wife gives birth to his child." Grandpa concludes that he and Grandma grew up through the birth of their children. He often thought of the old saying, "Where there is no pain, there is no gain." Character is molded in the fiery furnace of pain and suffering. God's greatest revelation of his own character is seen in the suffering and death of His Son on the cross.

Changes began to take place in Grandpa's and Grandma's household with a two year old and a new baby. The two year old got less attention from Grandma (So did Grandpa). Learning to share Grandma was not without its problems. Life was much more complicated with more mouths to feed, more clothes to be washed, and two babies to diaper and bathe. Sometimes both babies would cry at the same time, and Grandma would have one and Grandpa the other. To make matters more complicated, there was only one rocker. Walking the floor with a baby is more tiring than rocking. Responsibilities were doubled and life was not easy, but Grandpa said, "It is good." The harder and more complicated things became, the more Grandpa whistled and sang. Grandma and Grandpa worked hard and prayed often.

Grandpa says, "We were discovering one of life's greatest truths. Happiness is not found in achieving goals or arriving at a particular destination. Happiness and meaning are found in the journey itself. As we accepted and shared responsibility together, we became a family. We discovered that in being part of a family who loved and forgave each others' sins and failures, we were discovering satisfaction and security. We were learning to grow in grace, knowledge and wisdom.

Grandpa says, "We were also discovering that babies are like sunshine, they just keep coming." In 1942, Grandpa and Grandma moved from their old hometown to

Louisville, Kentucky, where Grandpa had a new job with the Murphy Elevator Company. This company built passenger and freight elevators, and at that time were making parts for the Army. This was a completely new experience for Grandma and Grandpa and the two young boys. It was like a second honeymoon for Grandpa and Grandma. They wanted a baby girl and often expressed this in front of the boys. Both boys wanted a little sister. Grandpa cast his vote and made it unanimous. Without family and friends, they had more time for each other and plenty of time to make love. Miracle of miracles, you guessed right, Grandma was soon pregnant for the third time. (Grandpa thought he and Grandma were doing pretty well in helping God with his creative plan). They were both elated, and Grandma knew it was going to be a little girl.

They located a new woman doctor in Camp Taylor, not far from where they lived. She was an excellent doctor, and they both felt comfortable with her. Things were working out well as they adjusted to a new community and a new church family.

Louisville was a very old and interesting city. In many ways, it was more like a big country town than an urban area. People were friendly, and it was easy to get acquainted and make new friends. Grandpa and Grandma had an opportunity to visit the popular Churchill Downs. They enjoyed seeing the beautiful and fast horses. (Grandpa also noticed a lot of beautiful women). Grandpa called to mind something his father often said, "Kentucky is the home of beautiful horses and fast women." After living there for a few years, Grandpa thought his father was right on target. They also visited the historic Bardstown Cathedral and admired its magnificent architecture and enjoyed the many paintings of the old masters that were on display.

Nine months passed very quickly. Grandma gave birth to a healthy baby girl. The doctor placed the beautiful little girl in Grandma's arms, saying, "Here is the little girl you have been wanting." Grandma, still weak and groggy said to her, "Doctor you're not kidding are you? I sure don't feel like any kidding right now." The doctor assured her that she indeed had a little baby girl. Grandpa stood by in admiration and was nearly overwhelmed when the doctor placed the soft little bundle in his arms. A few minutes later Grandpa hurried to the telephone to call members of Grandma's family, and his family, to share their new-found joy in a baby girl. At home, the two boys were fascinated by their little sister. She added charm and beauty to the growing family circle. The boys loved to hold her, and they thought it was real cool when she gurgled and cooed.

Grandpa was working twelve to fifteen hours a day and seven days a week at the elevator company where they were making products for the Army and Navy during World War II. Grandpa neither had the time or energy to help care for the baby as much as he would have liked. However, Grandma proved equal to the task and loved every minute of caring for her daughter and the two boys. Grandma took great pride in raising her three children. Grandma understood full well that God's creative process was not only a matter of having babies, but it was also necessary to provide an atmosphere of love in which the children could develop and grow into mature men and women.

Several weeks before Christmas, Grandpa started building the boys two large army trucks with ball bearing wheels. The trucks were made to scale. Grandpa painted them just as real army trucks were painted and placed the official insignias on each side. On Christmas morning the boys were elated, and Grandpa was filled with pride as he watched them sit on their trucks and ride them down the walk in front of their apartment. What a joy to have a family where there is fun and love.

There was never a dull moment in Grandpa's family, for change was an ever present reality. Grandpa says, "If you can't make peace with change, you are dead and you don't know it." He continues, "Change is written into the very nature of God's universe."

Grandpa was soon to have a far-reaching, life changing experience that placed the family in completely new and different surroundings. Grandpa experienced a personal relationship to God through Jesus Christ in a very meaningful way. Grandpa says, "I was born into a Christian home, always loved the church, and believed in God. However, this experience was different. This new relationship was personal and changed the whole direction and purpose of my life. Consequently, it changed the lives of every member of my family."

Since the earliest recollections of his childhood, Grandpa had felt the call to Christian ministry. This new experience vividly reminded him of that neglected call. The time for decision had arrived. Grandpa felt the call to ministry was first a call to preparation, a call to special education. The decision meant leaving a high paying job and the beautiful apartment and what seemed to be a wonderful life style.

Grandpa was a machinist and toolmaker at the elevator where he had become a foreman and a consultant. His salary was unbelievable because of the high demand for skilled toolmakers during the war.

The decision made, the family moved to Wilmore, Kentucky, where Grandpa entered and graduated from Asbury College, and later graduated from Garrett Biblical Institute, a seminary on the campus of Northwestern University in Evanston, Illinois. This was a gigantic step and was taken only after much prayer and careful consideration. After all, it is no ordinary thing to quit a high paying job to enter college at the age of 27 with three children to feed and clothe. Some of Grandpa's friends, including the executives at the elevator company, thought Grandpa had flipped his lid.

The family moved into an apartment in what had formerly been an old hotel in Wilmore. It was a dilapidated, old, two story frame house that was a complete contrast to the lovely apartment from which they moved. Grandma never complained, for they were still madly in love, and seeking to discover the meaning of life. Grandma and Grandpa were on a long journey and felt God was leading them. Even though things were often difficult, they never looked back but moved persistently forward.

Grandpa took an appointment with the Kentucky Conference of the Methodist Church. The two churches paid a sum total of $465.00 per year. There was no mileage allowance, and the family had to drive over 50 miles each way every Sunday. Grandpa had made six times that much in a month at the elevator. Grandpa knew that $465.00 a year was not sufficient to provide for the needs of the family. Grandpa had an unshakable faith that God would somehow show him how to make ends meet if he kept doing the best he could.

Hard work best characterizes the next few months of Grandpa and Grandma's lives. They both went to work scrubbing the walls and windows, the ceiling and floors in every room of the old hotel. Each room was painted and completely redecorated. Grandpa and Grandma did all the work, and they used up what little savings they had accumulated. (One good thing, they had plenty of room). A girl whom they knew from Louisville was entering college and could not get a room in the dormitory. She rented one of the bedrooms. This provided much needed income. When it seemed they would not have sufficient funds for their needs, things always seemed to work out. It was hard work, more than either had ever done before, but they were on an exciting journey that filled their lives with joy and meaning. The journey was long and hard, but they discovered they were never alone.

Grandpa says, "God never promised the journey would be easy, but he did promise, 'I will be with you.'"

This was a period of difficult adjustments. The kids enrolled in school and adjusted well to the community. Grandpa enrolled in college and loved his classes and the stimulation of his mind. Grandpa got a job in a grocery store after school and on Saturdays. Each Sunday the family would drive 50 miles to the two little churches. Each week the churches would hand him $9.00 in cash as pay for that week. Grandpa would hand them back .90 cents, a tithe, as was his custom. Grandma would watch, and then on the way home would say, "We are going to starve if you keep tithing." Grandpa would answer, "If we can't live on $8.10 with the Lord's blessing, we can't live on the $9.00 without his blessings." Grandma and the kids went with Grandpa every Sunday, even though they had to leave home at 7:00 a.m. and would not return until 10:30 p.m. The churches had an evening service as well as a Sunday morning worship service. Grandma was a real trooper, and walked side by side with Grandpa every step of the long journey. Grandpa says, "It took grace, grit and gumption. Grandma was a great mother to her children and was Grandpa's best friend through all the difficult and frustrating times. However, they were happy because they were following their dreams. They experienced the joy of the journey as they followed what they believed was God's

plan for their lives. Grandpa says, "Meaning and fulfillment best describes the emotion we felt."

As would be expected, they still found time to make
love, in spite of the hard work and adjustments. You
guessed it right again! Grandma became pregnant for the
fourth and final time. Grandpa began to think, plan and
pray, about providing more income. There was a real need
for student housing in Wilmore. Grandpa knew there were
going to be doctor and hospital bills. There would be one
more mouth to feed, along with other growing expenses
and responsibilities. Grandpa says: "Sometimes I became
frightened and frustrated by the overwhelming responsibilities of providing for my growing family while trying to
get an education. I would grow angry and fuss with God.
Then a passage of scripture would come from my subconscious mind, 'I can do all things through Christ.' I would
remember that I was not alone; both God and Grandma
were on my side. (Who could ask for anything more?) I
would then move steadily forward." The time had come for
practical planning and action.

Grandpa bought a large house. The college dormitory
housing was very limited, and the need for off-campus
housing was great. Even though Grandma was pregnant,
she worked very hard fixing up the old house. Some days
while Grandpa was in class she would paint an entire room
and have it all completed and cleaned up by the time
Grandpa got home. They did all the work and did not hire
anyone. It is well within the mark to say Grandma did
more work on the old house than Grandpa. There was
work and more work. They both persevered, and by the
beginning of the second quarter the house was completed
redecorated and ready to rent. The rooms filled immediately and the income was welcome. Grandpa says, "God provides well for those who are willing to work."

The new income was a lifesaver. Along with the money Grandpa made at the grocery store and received from the churches he served, they were able to live well. Grandpa was able to continue his education. Even so, there was a constant battle of the budget. Unexpected sources of income were serendipity and helped make ends meet. There were not many grants or scholarships in those days.

Grandpa says, "We did not have much money, but we were never poor. We were rich in God's grace."

There were financial woes ahead for the family in spite of Grandpa's faith and both Grandpa and Grandma's hard work. But Grandpa kept on preaching his beliefs, and persevering.

A Christian doctor in Louisville heard Grandpa preach a sermon in the Victory Center in Louisville, Kentucky (a ministry to servicemen). He was so moved and touched by God that he sent a $2000.00 check to Asbury College and had it deposited in Grandpa's account, unknown to Grandpa. Grandpa was about to drop out of school for a quarter because of the lack of funds. Grandpa fussed and prayed and even became angry with God. Grandpa felt God had let him down. The business manager of the college came to see Grandpa and inquired as to why he had not registered. Grandpa told him he was just going to lay out for a quarter. The business manager wanted to know if it was because of finance, and said, "You have been one of our finest and most dedicated student pastors. You must have a reason." Grandpa was embarrassed and lied about it and said, "No, I just want to rest for a quarter." The business manager then told him about the two thousand dollars that was in his account. He said, "The doctor deposited it in your account two months ago, and requested we not tell you until you really needed it." Grandpa could hardly believe what he heard. He thanked the business manager over and over again. After he was gone, Grandpa fell on his knees and prayed that God would forgive him for fussing about something God had taken care of two months before. Grandpa was ashamed of having so little faith, for lying and growing angry. He thanked God for His great love and benevolent care. The next day he registered for the semester, even though he was a day late. Life was good. Unexpected sources of income reminded Grandpa and Grandma that they were never alone as they walked this journey of faith. Grandpa says, "We were learning that God never gives us all we want, when we want it, but he does bless us with all we need and 'exceedingly abundantly above all that we ask or think.'"

Grandma survived all the hard work on the old house and in the early morning hours of March 16, 1947, she awakened Grandpa at 2 a.m., informing him that she was in labor. After calling the doctor, they bundled up, got into the car and drove sixteen miles to the Good Samaritan Hospital in Lexington, Kentucky. A light snow was falling, which made the drive more nerve-racking. They arrived at 3 a.m. and Grandma was taken into the delivery room.

Grandpa nervously made his way to the designated waiting room where another expectant father was pacing the floor. The man said, "I have been here since yesterday afternoon at 3:30 p.m. I sure hope you don't have to wait that long." Grandpa took a seat and started reading a magazine. The other man continued to walk the floor. About 10 minutes later, a nurse entered the waiting room. The man jumped up expecting the long-awaited news. The nurse turned to Grandpa saying, "You have a fine son, and your wife is doing fine." Grandpa felt sorry for the other man but was glad for the good news.

The nurse escorted Grandpa to Grandma's bedside. She was holding the baby in her arms and started crying. They both cried tears of joy. Grandpa took his son up in his arms and gently kissed him. By 5 a.m. he was on his way home. He got there in time to fix breakfast for the kids, before getting them ready for school. They were a happy bunch of kids, and the students living in the house seemed to rejoice as much as the rest of the family. They had become Grandpa and Grandma's extended family.

After the kids were off to school, Grandpa had time to reflect on all that had happened in such a short period of time. He smiled when he thought of what the doctor said, "You two seem to gets things done in a hurry." Grandpa thought of how clever God was when he conceived the idea of how to replenish the earth's population, and included Grandpa and Grandma in the process. He sat there and laughed and said to himself, "I bet God is laughing too." Grandpa also thinks God applauds when people really enjoy their sex life in marriage; after all, he created it.

Grandpa often says, "The creative process is so incredible that it had to be conceived in the mind of God."

A celebration and a consultation were in order when Grandma and the baby arrived home from the hospital. Grandpa and Grandma, the kids, and the students who lived in the house, all thanked God for the healthy little newcomer who had joined the family circle.

Grandpa and Grandma had a consultation and came to a consensus that they had done their part in helping God with the creative process. There would be no more babies! Grandpa said, "Enough is enough!" Grandpa and Grandma decided that it was time to enjoy life by providing a loving atmosphere in their home where their children could feel secure and grow into normal, well-rounded, healthy adults. To that end, they were committed.

Grandpa thinks God looked on and said, "Good, at least they are learning a few things as they grow up together."

The time has come to let others share in the joy and responsibility of bringing new life into the world. Grandpa and Grandma knew that in due time their children would begin to take up where they left off. Grandpa and Grandma would be blessed with grandchildren and great-grandchildren. All this has proved to be true, as babies just keep coming... like sunshine. Grandpa and Grandma knew that the twofold task of caring for their four children and preparing for the ministry would be all they could handle. They felt both tasks were God's will for their lives.

Grandpa says, "We stood in awe and wonder as God's plan continued to unfold along the way on our journey."

The student renters were elated by the addition of the new baby. They had a party and brought gifts for him. One of the boys entertained the kids by removing his right eye. None of the family had known that he had a glass eye as a result of an accident early in his life. The kids thought it was really cool when he suddenly popped out his eye. They shouted with glee, "Do it again!" They also begged him to teach them how to take out their eye. Now the student had some teaching to do in order to keep them from harming their own eyes.

The baby remained the center of attention and with nine other people in the house, he became spoiled, to say the least. Grandpa and Grandma were learning that they were not only lovers, they were becoming "best friends." Grandpa says, "If a marriage is to survive, it is essential that the partners do become best friends."

There was one problem in the creative process. God made Adam and Eve in His own image, and that included the power of choice. This meant that all their offspring who followed also had the power to choose.

The gift of freedom is inherent in the creative process. The root of our personal and social evil grows out of a misuse of God's gift of freedom. The gift of freedom has the potential for good or evil. It is as you choose!

Adam and Eve "blew it." God placed them in the garden of Eden and gave them every kind of tree and shrub one can imagine. There was every kind of fruit and vegetable to provide them with food. He gave them only one rule to keep. (Wow! Can you imagine having only one rule to obey?) God said, "You may eat freely of every tree in the garden, but of the tree of knowledge of good and evil you shall not eat. . . " Therein lay the problem.

This one rule was the precise point where Adam and Eve got into trouble, and in doing so got us all in a heap big mess. They were disobedient and did exactly what God told them not to do, and in so doing opened the door for sin and evil in the world. They lost their innocence and intimate relationship with God. They had to move "East of Eden."

Grandpa says, "I am not sure how this all happened, but I know for sure it is a picture of what is still happening. Men and women have been disobedient ever since and as a consequence are paying a terrible price."

Grandpa continues, "I know only that this is a perfect picture of how men and women act today. It is a timeless photograph of our society." Adam and Eve:

"Blew it."

"Covered it up."

"Blamed someone else."

"Were separated from God."

The one thing Adam and Eve were not free to do was to escape the consequences of their own sins. Each one was responsible, and each of them shared the guilt and the consequences.

Grandpa says, "Every tub must sit on its own bottom at the judgment."

This picture flashes before people's eyes every day.

It teaches us that there is no freedom without responsibility! Benjamin Franklin once said, "My freedom to swing my fist ends where another man's nose begins." We can never understand freedom outside responsible relationships with God and our neighbor. This is graphically illustrated every day in politics, the business world, and yes, even in the church.

While serving as a District Superintendent in the United Methodist Church, Grandpa observed a number of good men, who spent at least seven years in higher education training for the ministry who "blew it." They lost their profession, and their families, in a moment of temptation. They could not escape responsibility and the consequences of their own actions. The same thing happened to men even in high offices in the church. The consequences of their actions left a string of broken hearts, wives, children, parents, and disillusioned congregations. They were free to yield to temptation, but were not free to escape the consequences.

Grandpa says, "This is why we need a Savior. None of us is without sin. Some of our sins and failures are not quite so apparent."

Compassion, and not criticism, is always in order under such circumstances. Grandpa always felt compassion for the person and his family, as well as the congregation.

It is time for confession! Grandpa faced and felt the same temptations. Grandpa says, "I was always glad that Grandma was aware when I was tempted. She seemed to have extrasensory perception or radar that detected when I was attracted to another woman. She would quickly and effectively put 'blinders' on me and tighten the reins." Grandpa always regretted when he was tempted and asked God to forgive him for hurting Grandma. Sometimes he wished he were not so human. However, he felt that he learned, from his own weakness, to empathize and understand the problems of others who were not so fortunate. Grandpa often says, "There go I but for the Grace of God and Grandma."

Grandpa says, "The church I love has spent thousands of hours and thousands of dollars arguing about lifestyles and trying to pass resolutions and legislation only to wind up exactly where they were when they started. That time and money could have been spent in more meaningful and productive ways. It is time to quit arguing and wasting time and money. It is time to take a long hard look at God's creative process and realize you cannot legislate or force responsible use of this great gift of God in relationships. The church needs to remind people they are free to choose their life style, but they are not free from the consequences of their own actions."

Grandpa says, "It is as you choose."

People must never take themselves too seriously. It is time to laugh!

A young teacher asked the boys and girls in her class to make up a rhyme about what they wanted to be when they grew up. They made the following contributions:

Little Mary said:

> When I grow to be a lady
> I want to have a baby
> If I can, and I think I can!

Little Johnnie said:

> When I grow to be a man
> I want to go to Japan
> If I can, and I think I can!

Little Jimmie said:

> When I grow to be a man
> to heck with Japan
> I want to help Mary with her little plan
> If I can, and I think I can!

The creative process is well and alive! It is everyone's responsibility to be a role model on how to use it and not abuse it in responsible relationships.

Grandpa says, "What a glorious privilege it is to help God with His plan to recreate life. We are not worthy nor do we deserve this sacred role. It is God's gift of grace! It has been a great motivating force in my life and has kept me ticking for 80 years.

Grandpa says: "Wonder is life, as seen through the eyes of a child."

CHAPTER 2
CEASELESS WONDERS

Grandpa says, "Come share my journey as we walk through the wonders of my childhood! We will have fun!"

As a three year old boy, Grandpa was brought to the business district on Good Hope Street in Cape Girardeau, Mo. Hundreds of people were milling about celebrating Armistice at the close of World War I in 1919. A huge celebration was taking place, with a marching band and soldiers in uniform. People were throwing paper streamers from the second floor of stores and office buildings. They were singing patriotic and popular war songs and shouting at the top of their voices. Policemen were riding their well-groomed horses One of the policemen, a friend of Grandpa's family, took three year old grandpa from the arms of his father and placed him in front of him on the horse and let him ride for a short distance. Grandpa says, "My childish heart filled with joy." People were overjoyed that peace had come to their troubled world, and they knew their loved ones would soon be coming home." Grandpa says, "This incredible picture was indelibly stamped on my young mind, never to be erased by time." Grandpa often thinks of this graphic scene and concludes that peace has been and always will be a worthy lifetime priority. The pursuit of "peace on earth and goodwill among men" shapes and motivates Grandpa's everyday life.

There was a building that stood gracefully at the back of the lot on which Grandpa's boyhood home was built. It was surrounded by fruit trees and flowers. For many, it would have been something to be endured. As a small boy, Grandpa saw it as a place of beauty, a sanctuary for meditation, a seat of learning, and a stimulator of his vivid imagination. It also filled a very necessary function for the family. In case you are wondering, it is an outdoor "privy." (Sometimes called a "two holer.") Grandpa calls it a "priceless privy."

This building had a particular significance for Grandpa because his father built it. One thing Grandpa loved was a five-pointed star that his father had cut out at the top of the door. It provided light for reading and brought the ever-widening horizons of the world into Grandpa's growing understanding.

The privy was also air conditioned. In each gable end, there was an opening near the top that let in the cool air and let out odors. These openings, along with the star, were covered with screen wire to keep out insects and other unwanted pests. Nothing was spared in order to provide comfort and convenience for all who used this facility. The star still fills Grandpa's life with a never-ending source of wonder.

Good reading was provided! This hall of learning had an excellent library where you could always find something interesting to read or pictures to enjoy! A basket filled with reading materials sat at each end of the privy in front of the seats.

Among the literary treasures placed in the baskets were such things as a <u>Sears and Roebuck</u> catalogue, an almanac' and a <u>Lancaster Seed Company</u> catalogue. There were also a number of daily newspapers, including the <u>St. Louis Post Dispatch</u> (Republican), <u>The Southeast Missourian</u>, <u>The St. Louis Globe Democrat</u>, plus a number of excellent magazines including the Saturday Evening Post, a real source of art because of the Norman C. Rockwell pictures.

Grandpa never spent a dull moment in the privy. He was fascinated by the pictures in the <u>Sears and Roebuck </u>catalogue that advertised everything from women's lingerie to men's boots. Grandpa first learned what girls were like and the clothes they wore, including lingerie. (There was no TV with bedroom scenes showing women wearing lingerie, and sometimes not any clothes at all.) Grandpa says, "I think in some instances the privy education was of a higher quality and more interesting than TV." Grandpa still appreciates good taste in clothing for both women and men. Grandpa says, "My appreciation for the arts started in the privy library and has continued to grow through the years."

It was in the "privy" that Grandpa became aware of the joy and rewards of becoming a good salesman. In the <u>Lancaster Seed Catalogue</u> he discovered that they gave prizes for selling their garden seed. Even though Grandpa was only five, he reasoned that all his neighbors purchased garden seed. He dreamed of having a wristwatch, a pocketknife, and a billfold. He sent in an order for seeds and sold them very quickly. He sent for a larger order and sold them all. He was soon the proud owner of a wristwatch, billfold and pocketknife. He was the envy of all the kids in the neighborhood. It made Grandpa feel very good, and he became more self-confident. It is a wonderful feeling to know that you can earn these things as the result of your own efforts.

One day Grandpa picked up The Globe Democrat and found they were giving away a coaster wagon called the 49th Street Flyer for selling subscriptions to their paper. He ordered the sales material and went to work. (He did not have enough sense to know that you could not sell a Democratic paper in a predominantly Republican community). In a six months' period he became the proud owner of the first 49th Street Flyer in his community. Grandpa was elated!

He sold many boxes of Cloverine Salve, a cure-all for cuts, bruises, and any other ailment you might have. Grandpa says, "One of the most important lessons I learned in the privy was the joy of being a salesman. It helped me throughout my entire life."

Grandpa says, "There are three basic rules to follow if you want to be a salesperson:

Know your product

Make the calls

Close the deal."

At 80 years of age, Grandpa still loves to sell. Grandpa says, "I first fell in love with the art of selling in my childhood seat of learning, the priceless privy."

Grandpa became an avid reader in the "privy." He still loves to read in the bathroom. During all the years that followed, there has always been a basket with reading material that you can reach without getting off the stool. It is a carry-over from a habit formed in the privy. This has helped to keep Grandpa's mind alive and well at 80. Grandpa says, "The privy is a part of the stuff of my life, and I shall ever be grateful."

Grandpa says, "It is easy for parents to get lost from their children." One day Grandpa's parents could not find him. They looked everywhere. The more they looked, the more concerned they became. After an hour of fruitless search, they alerted the neighbors who joined in the hunt, to no avail! They then notified the police.

After asking many questions, the officer took up the search. He saw the "privy" and walked toward it. He stood in front of the door and noticed the button on the inside was fastened. He took out his pocketknife, slipped it through the crack between the door and the casing and turned the little button that fastened it from the inside. The door swung open, and there sat Grandpa on his throne with his head against the wall. He was sound asleep, unaware of all the excitement, in his sanctuary of safety. His mother grabbed him up in her arms and kissed him. He blinked his eyes and smiled. He was unaware that anything was happening. His dad hugged him, and the neighbors and friends rejoiced with them. Grandpa says, "It is so easy for parents to get lost from a child."

Is a "privy" an inconvenience or an asset? You figure it out! Grandpa says, "My life is richer and fuller because of a small white building on the back of the lot of my childhood home " Some may think of the "privy" as something to be tolerated, but to Grandpa it will always be remembered as an asset that still influences his daily life. It is a never-ending wonder that is a part of the stuff of his life.

Some things are stamped indelibly on the mind of a small child, and that child is affected consciously or subconsciously forever. Grandpa says, "That is true of the following experiences I had as a small lad." An evangelist had come to the Maple Avenue Methodist Church to conduct a two-week nightly series of services. Grandpa attended each night with his parents. Some nights he would get so tired he would go to sleep on the pew between his parents with his head on his dad's lap. One night the wife of the evangelist drew a picture of the cross. The lights were lowered and a spotlight played on the drawing. As she drew, her husband sang "The Old Rugged Cross," and talked about how Christ died on the cross and how much he loved us. Grandpa says, "Tears flowed down my cheeks, and I made a decision that I wanted to follow this strange man on the cross and to be like him." Grandpa did not comprehend the implications of the decision he made, and he did not always follow Christ. But, he never forgot that moving experience and how it affected him the rest of his life.

God said, "Let there be light," and there was light in the tail of a firefly. As a small boy, Grandpa was intrigued by the firefly. Grandpa says, "My little sister and I would catch them and place them in a fruit jar with holes in the lid in order for them to get air. "He and his sister were fascinated as they watched them produce a silent Fourth of July display. Grandpa believes the firefly silently punctuates the dark moments of our lives with a reminder of God's neverending love. We may not always see them, but their intermittent rays of light come to us at unexpected times.

Grandpa would catch June bugs and tie a thread to their legs, hold the loose end of the string, and watch them fly. They were more fun than modern day model airplanes. You never had to buy batteries, and furthermore they did not cost a penny. Grandpa says, "The world of nature has an inherent Toys "R" Us store for those who have an imagination."

Have you every watched a spider spin a web? Have you ever watched it roll the web up in the face of a storm?

It will amaze you if you watch an army of ants work their fetes of cooperative achievements.

Grandpa says, "These lessons from nature have made a major contribution to my life. This is the stuff that has shaped my life."

Grandpa says, "Storms have serendipity." Wonderful things are often found in the aftermath of a storm. One day Grandpa discovered a baby red-headed woodpecker. It had been thrown out of the nest when the tree in which it was located blew down. Grandpa gathered it up, wrapped it in his handkerchief, and took it home. With the help of his mother, he fed the baby bird worms and insects and nurtured the bird until it could fly. Some of his friends informed him that a woodpecker could not be tamed.

However, the bird became a pet. The woodpecker would eat out of Grandpa's hand and light on his shoulder. When the bird began to fly, it would take short trips, but always return. Everyone loved "Woody" (as he was affectionately named), and he became a part of the family for two years.

When the family took a trip, Woody went with them. Grandpa had a little box with vents in which Woody traveled. While visiting a county fair in Anna, Illinois, Woody got lost. Grandpa released him for exercise and play. At first he would fly a few minutes and return to Grandpa's shoulder. In the strange surroundings, and with so many unfamiliar people, he became frightened, flew away and was not able to find his way back. After waiting and watching for a long time, Grandpa had to give up. Grandpa was really shook up and grieved for many days. Grandpa says, "I learned a valuable lesson. Pets are wonderful companions and when you lose one, it brings pain and sorrow, just as losing a member of your family."

"He was a dog and a half long and a half dog high." That is the way Grandpa's father described Teddy. Teddy was Grandpa's first dog. "This," Grandpa said, "was a fitting description." Teddy had no pedigree, and his only claim to fame was his unique shape and his love and loyalty to Grandpa. He was just a plain old dog with a warm heart and a wagging tail. The two became inseparable, and wherever Grandpa went there you would find Teddy. Blue Bell Island was their favorite spot. They often hiked to the Island that was about a mile and a half from home. The Island was paradise in Grandpa and Teddy's eyes. It was covered with beautiful blue bells that grew along the banks of Cape LaCroix creek. For some reason, at some point in time, the creek divided and surrounded a large piece of ground, forming an island. The water flowed around each side of the land, and then rejoined at the southernmost point. Grandpa and Teddy would gather great armloads of blue bells and take them home to "Mom."

On one side of the Island was a large, deep hole of water that provided a great place to swim on warm days. A large tree limb extended out over the water from a high bank on one side. Grandpa tied a strong rope to the limb, and then tied a handle to the bottom of the rope about four feet above the water. He would swing off the bank out over the water and drop. Teddy was always waiting for him in the water.

A mud slide provided fun galore. Grandpa and Teddy would race to the top of the high bank with Grandpa carrying an old bucket filled with water from the creek. Grandpa would pour the water on the mud slide. They would repeat this several times. Then both of them would jump onto the slide and down the bank and go into the cool water. They would race back to the top for a repeat performance! What fun and excitement they enjoyed! No modern amusement park can offer as much fun for a boy and his dog. Grandpa always says, "Joyful rewards await those who have eyes to see and discover nature's amusement parks, and it is all free." Grandpa believes heaven will have a Blue Bell island for himself and Teddy.

Grandpa and Teddy enjoyed another happy and rewarding pastime in nearby Houck's woods that adjoined the island. Grandpa built rabbit traps from scrap lumber available from his father's building projects. The traps were basically a four-sided, oblong box with a trapdoor. Grandpa made a wooden trigger that ran from the door to the back of the trap on top of the box. The trigger was balanced over a forked stick, and a second piece of wood with a notch went down through the hole in the top of the box and descended into the box until it was only about an inch from the bottom where cabbage or lettuce was placed as bait. This enticed the rabbits to enter the trap. The rabbit would nibble on the bait, trip the trigger, and the trapdoor would fall, cutting off the escape.

Grandpa and Teddy would set four or five traps along the trails in the afternoon. Early the next day they would run the traps and usually get two or three rabbits on late Fall mornings. Grandpa was always proud when they showed up on the family table. Sometimes they would give a rabbit to an elderly neighbor in the community. It was a joyful experience that cemented the relationship between a boy and his dog.

There were other thriving enterprises on Blue Bell Island and in Houck woods! Sassafras grew in abundance in both places. The roots were used to make a delicious "healthy choice" tea. Grandpa and Teddy would dig the roots, take them home, cut them into short pieces, and wash them thoroughly. The roots were then tied in small bunches and sold to neighbors and local grocery stores for five cents per packet. Teddy always accompanied Grandpa, and when someone made a purchase he would politely wag his tail to express his thanks! This drew Grandpa and Teddy closer together and provided Grandpa with spending money.

When Teddy died, Grandpa grieved for days. Many days of adventure and excitement had established a deep and fulfilling relationship. Teddy's death left a great void in Grandpa's life. The memories of those wonderful days of companionship still bring a warm feeling of gratitude and shape Grandpa's life. Grandpa says, "Teddy's love and devotion will always live in my heart."

Teddy's death taught Grandpa many things about suffering and sorrow. It gave him an understanding of what people feel in the loss of a family member. He could empathize with them and help them to learn from the experience. It enabled him to communicate hope for the future. It made him a better minister of Jesus Christ.

Grandpa does not think of these events in a nostalgic way but sees them as dynamic and potent motivators that stimulate his thoughts, the words he writes, and dictate what he is now doing. Grandpa says, "A 'privy' and a 'pet' called 'Teddy' are definitely woven into the fabric of my being, though I am 80 years young." THE WONDERS OF CHILDHOOD NEVER END! THEY ARE CEASELESS!

Old Fort "D" was a land of fantasy! Here Grandpa spent many hours of his childhood. Fort "D" was the largest of four Civil War forts built in Cape Girardeau, in response to an order issued by Ulysses S. Grant in 1861. Fort "D" was located south of St. Vincent's College on a low bluff overlooking the Mississippi River on the south side of the city. The view of the river gave protection from confederates coming up the river from the south or from Arkansas.

Grandpa's home was only a few blocks from the fort, and he and his friends spent many enjoyable hours playing war in this land of enchantment. Missouri, as a state, was divided. Residents were never quite sure whether they should support the Union or the Confederacy. This was still true among Grandpa's playmates. One of his neighbors was a strong sympathizer of the Confederates, and Grandpa was a loyal supporter of the Union. The kids would choose sides, and the war was on.

The Old Fort (that's what everyone called it) was surrounded by large mounds of dirt and trenches, originally built to be low rifle pits. They were built for protection and were covered with grass in Grandpa's time. The Old Fort had a large supply of hedge-apples. The boys used them for cannonballs, and there was ample supply for both sides. The dirt bluff on the east side, overlooking the river, was covered with bushes and small trees. Both sides would dig caves in the banks where they would hide and avoid "the enemy."

Grandpa, like all the rest of the kids, got hit many times by a cannonball and rolled from the top of the bluff to the bottom. (You were really never accepted as a full-fledged soldier until you were blown off the top of the bluff). Sometimes minor injuries were sustained.

The boys set up a hospital in the center of the Fort to minister to the wounded from both sides (This seemed appropriate since the soldiers from both sides were friends and neighbors just as they were in the days of the Civil War). Grandpa says, "This is the wonderful stuff that is embedded in my guts."

Here in the Old Fort, history came to life. Grandpa learned more about the history of the Civil War in this land of fantasy than he did in school. Grandpa says, "I learned that history is not boring facts about the past, but a dynamic flow of energy from real live people of one generation to the next." The people in our past determine, in part, what we are today. It is the stuff that produces our future. Grandpa says, "After playing war on the Old Fort D, I believe more than ever that peace is a pearl of great price, worthy of a lifetime commitment. No one wins in war."

It is time for school. Grandpa was wearing new pants, shirt and tie. (They were all made by his mom). His shoes were shined and his hair brushed and combed. He was groomed as near to perfection as was possible for a five year old boy. Grandpa had been looking forward to this, his first day of school, with great expectation. This was also the opening day for the new May Greene School. The school was only a few blocks from Grandpa's home. As he neared the school, Grandpa grew frightened and thought about turning around and heading for home, but he kept going.

As Grandpa walked along, an older neighbor boy came up beside him and walked with him. He didn't want the boy to know he was frightened, so he tried not to let it show. The boy walked with Grandpa to the school door. When they went in, the boy directed him to the first grade classroom. (Grandpa often wonders if the boy knew how much he had helped him). The room was filled with boys and girls who were about his age. He knew several of the children, and this made him feel better.

When the teacher came into the room, she introduced herself and asked each one around the room to stand and give his/her name. Grandpa was in the second row and stood to state his name. The teacher smiled and commented on his clothes. Grandpa proudly blurted out, "My mom made them. Even the tie."

Unnoticed, the principal of the new school entered the room and observed the procedure. After all the children had finished giving their names, the teacher introduced Miss Alma, the principal, who made an announcement and assured the students of her friendship and support. Before leaving, Miss Alma asked the classroom teacher if Grandpa could accompany her as she made her rounds to the different classrooms. As they visited each class, she made her announcement, and then stood Grandpa on the teacher's desk saying, "This is my new friend from the first grade. I wanted you to meet him and see his new clothes his mother made." There was applause in every room. Grandpa really felt good. Grandpa says, "That day, I fell in love with schools and teachers and forever after I have been a ham."

After that unusual experience, Grandpa had no fear of school, he loved it. He now had a friend who was in charge of the school, and she was a very down-to-earth person. Most of the other students in the upper grades now knew his name, and he made many close friends. May Greene was now his school, and he belonged. Grandpa says, "From this experience I learned to love teachers, and it fanned the desire to learn. That desire is still burning at 80."

Grandpa says, "An elephant can be a real embarrassment." Each year the May Greene School produced a three-ring circus for the parents and community. Boys and girls participated in filling all the roles, including the ringmaster and all the animals. The teachers were directors and facilitators. Grandpa was chosen to walk under the rear end of an elephant, and a friend was to walk under the front end. "Wow! isn't that some role?" His favorite teacher did the recruiting. She said, "This is a very difficult role and not everyone can do it. It is just right for you." She was right about one thing, it was difficult. Grandpa could not refuse this teacher, though his better judgment told him it was a mistake. The body consisted of a wooden frame made in the shape of an elephant, trunk and all. The frame was covered with gray bunting to resemble elephant skin. The feet and legs of both boys were covered with the same material (a remarkable likeness to the real thing).

The role proved to be a very difficult task as it was dark under the frame, and the boys could not see each other's feet or where they were walking. For weeks, the teacher patiently tried to teach them how to walk in step with one another and in rhythm with the music being played during the performance. It was extremely hot, and the more the boys sweat the more frustrated they became. The teacher was very patient. Finally, the last week before the production, Grandpa and his friend seemed to be getting their act together. They were no longer stepping on one another, though they could not see each other's feet. The teacher was elated and praised them in front of the other performers. She reminded them of the importance of their role.

The day of production finally arrived. The gymnasium was packed, and the trumpets sounded the fanfare for the grand entrance of the ringmaster. Finally, the moment arrived, and the ringmaster announced the long-awaited entrance of Ellie, "the well-trained elephant from the far away jungles of Africa." Ellie would perform fetes that no other elephant in captivity had ever before attempted. The music was playing while Ellie marched to the center of the ring. Both boys stumbled, got their feet tangled, and nearly fell in the sawdust on the floor. They could never get back into step with the music. Grandpa stepped on his friend's heels several times. The teacher cried, the crowd roared and went wild with applause. Grandpa and his friend were embarrassed. Grandpa thought there was one good thing about the whole thing, no one could see them under the elephant. After it was over, Grandpa and his friend thought it was a lot of fun, and the audience really enjoyed it. This would be remembered for a long time to come. After the teacher had time to get everything into perspective, even she decided it was a good show. Grandpa says, "I learned to be very careful when someone is trying to recruit you for a role that is so important that no one else can do." (That is especially true if it means marching under the rear end of an elephant).

The teacher who recruited Grandpa for the elephant role was attractive, intelligent, very talented, and was the best teacher he ever knew. (In addition, she loved to trout fish). She was a music teacher who enriched Grandpa's life in many ways. Grandpa's love for music was instilled in him by his home, and his favorite teacher continued to cultivate his love for music. Miss Hazel introduced her students to Henry Wadsworth Longfellow's poem, "The Song of Hiawatha." This was an important Indian poem based on Hiawatha's life. Hiawatha was a Mohawk Chief who sought to promote universal peace among Indian tribes. The poem is in single line verse and tells of his birth, childhood, and wedding to Minnehaha. It tells of his life's work and shares his grief at the death of his wife and friends. It has great appeal because it runs the gamut of human emotion. It is a very lengthy work, and the teacher required her students to memorize large sections of the poem that she felt were significant. The haunting lines of the poem that Grandpa memorized often come to his mind:

> On the shores of Gittche Gumee,
> Of the shinning Big-Sea-Waters. ...

Grandpa remembers this poem and its meaningful messages about life as seen through the eyes of this Indian chief. Grandpa says, "I am thankful for my music teacher who required much of her students but gave more of herself."

Baseball players have a way of getting the attention of the American people. That was true when "Billy Sunday" came to Cape Girardeau and held evangelistic services when Grandpa was a small boy. Sunday was a converted professional baseball star who played for Chicago, Pittsburgh, and Philadelphia. He was born on a farm in Iowa and was raised in an orphanage. He was an ordained minister in the Presbyterian Church. Sunday used his baseball background to become a far-reaching evangelist.

The meeting in Cape Girardeau was held in a crude tabernacle that was built for the occasion on what was known as the Whitlow lot, a block north of Broadway. Church people from all denominations were organized and involved in preparation for the meeting. All around the city, cottage prayer meetings were held, and a spirit of expectancy and unity was created before the meeting started.

One evening Grandpa's folks took him to the service. It was an experience Grandpa will long remember. There was spirited and rousing singing, led by Homer Rodeheaver, who also sang touching solos. When Sunday got up to preach, things began to happen. It was a hot night, and Billy quickly shed his coat, rolled up his sleeves and went to work. Sunday raced to and fro across the platform. His voice was like a foghorn and could be heard in the far corners of the tabernacle. (There was no P.A. system, and none was needed). Billy got on his knees when he talked about prayer. Grandpa was fascinated. The language Billy Sunday used was plain and clear. Even a small boy got the message. It was a four-pronged message:

He was fighting sin.

All men have sinned.

Christ is the answer to sinners' needs.

All men can be saved through Christ.

Grandpa says, "Sunday made a deep and lasting impression on my life."

The harmonica added a new dimension to Grandpa's life. A member of a service club visited May Greene School and talked to the student body about participating in a boy's harmonica band they wanted to sponsor. Grandpa intermittently volunteered as did another 24 boys in the school. The service club gave each boy a Marine Band Harmonica, and instructions were given by one of the teachers. Grandpa fell in love with the instrument and practiced every day. He was soon playing old tunes such as "Turkey in the Straw" and other favorites. The band played for the Lions Club and other organizations. It was a fun experience.

Grandpa learned to whistle when he was very young, and it almost became an obsession. He nearly drove his parents up the wall as he practiced different sounds and styles of whistling. He would turn on the radio and listen to Elmo Tanner, the professional whistler with the Ted Weems band. Tanner had a unique style of warbling, and Grandpa learned to imitate him. Grandpa whistled when he was alone and walking home on a dark night. He found it gave him courage to whistle such songs as "What a Friend We Have in Jesus" or "Jesus Loves Me." Neighbors said, "We know what time Grandpa comes home each night because we hear him whistling." Grandpa found that whistling has many values. A task becomes lighter when you whistle as you work. Whistling can change negative thoughts into positive attitudes and actions. A drab life can be transformed into a joyous and productive life. Whistling can enrich a boring life and make it into a thrilling adventure. Whistling brings courage and strength in the face of danger and fear. Grandpa says, "Whistling motivates and keeps my life an adventure. It keeps me ticking!"

Grandpa says, "I hope whistling will be a part of the heritage I leave to my family. Nothing would make me happier than to have a bunch of kids, grandchildren, and great-grandchildren who would enrich their own lives and bless the world by being whistlers.

One day a large moving van backed up to a house in the neighborhood. As Grandpa watched them unload, he noticed a cute little girl with pigtails. (Grandpa always noticed pigtails). She was busy helping her mother with the many tasks of trying to get settled. Grandpa thought that this was something that required exploration. He went over and gave them a helping hand and managed to find something to do in the vicinity where the little girl was working. He found out her name was Patricia, and they called her "Pat." He managed to talk to her several times. Grandpa and Pat seemed to hit it off from the beginning and were soon friends.

The next morning he managed to get to the front walk just about the time Pat was coming out to go to school. They walked to school together, and Grandpa enjoyed showing her around the school and took her to her classroom. Grandpa had suddenly discovered a new world that included girls. He found that girls are more fun than boys, and he was deeply involved in his first puppy love affair.

Grandpa walked home with Pat, and they held hands. They got to her house all too quickly. She looked over at Grandpa and said, "l like you." Grandpa was walking on air as he made his way to his home. Grandpa said to himself, "Wow! Boy! This is living. She likes me!" He suddenly began to comb his hair and brushed his teeth more regularly. Grandpa wanted to look his best to impress the girl with pigtails who had him in a tailspin. Grandpa thought, "This is it; she will be my girl forever."

About a year later Grandpa was shocked when Pat told him her dad was being transferred to St. Louis, and they would be moving soon. St. Louis was 125 miles away. He would never see her again. They were both sad and very quiet as they walked home from school that last day. When they got to Pat's house, she suddenly reached over and kissed Grandpa on the cheek. His head was spinning, and his tongue was tied as he left her and made his way home. When the van pulled away the next day, the bottom seemed to drop out of Grandpa's world. He lived through it, and in a few days he was amazed at how many other little girls caught his eye. Grandpa says, "This experience taught me that boys and girls are compatible and that life is more fun when you include both in your circle of friends." God looked on and smiled saying, "At least he has enough sense to learn a few things about girls that I created."

When Grandpa started to school, his mom and dad warned him that he was not to get into fights. If he did, he would be punished when he got home. Grandpa says, "This always troubled me." There were a number of big bullies who lived in the area just south of Grandpa's home. One of them, named Jack, was supposed to be the toughest boy in May Greene School. He loved to pick on Grandpa and chase him home from school because he knew Grandpa would not fight. It was great sport for him, and it helped make all the other kids accept his authority over them. One warm day, Jack was chasing Grandpa home from school and calling him an SOB. Grandpa's dad was working on the roof of a house he was building and heard Jack calling Grandpa an SOB. This made him angry, and he yelled to Grandpa, "If you don't turn around and whip him, I am going to get down off this roof and thrash you soundly." That was all Grandpa needed. He reversed his course and quickly headed straight for Jack. Jack was so surprised that Grandpa knocked him down and gave him a good beating before he knew what was happening. Jack jumped up with a bloody nose and ran for home, with Grandpa chasing him and yelling, "If you ever call me that again, I will whip you until you can't run home."

Jack never chased Grandpa again. They became friends, and Grandpa was made a hero by the other students. Grandpa says, "I decided it may be necessary to protect yourself if you want to survive. However, I am not a fighter, I am a lover."

Grandpa grabbed two 2" x 2" upright pieces of wood about six feet long, got on the edge of the porch, stepped on cleats nailed or screwed to the uprights about three feet from the bottom. The uprights were then placed behind his arms, and away he would go, walking or running, feeling like a giant. He was walking on tall stilts that were products of his own hands. Many of the things Grandpa and his friends played with were homemade. Some of the stilts they made were short and close to the ground, while others were tall. These provided a variety of thrills. King of the stilts was a favorite pastime with Grandpa and the kids with whom he competed. They would bump each other, trying to knock one another off the stilts. The challenge was to see who could out-maneuver the others and remain standing. The last one standing on the stilts was the King. Many bruises and sore spots resulted from this sport, but it was a lot of fun and kept them busy for hours and out of trouble.

Grandpa says, "Homemade devices for recreation were a great source of fun." Pet Milk cans were used to make foot clogs. High jump and pole vault standards were built, and pits were dug and filled with sawdust, from the nearby Lemmings sawmill, to make the landing easier. Tree houses and swings of many varieties attested to his boyhood friends' ability to find ways to enjoy their youth.

While still in grade school, Grandpa became interested in building crystal set radios. Hirsch Brothers were the first to build a radio station in Cape Girardeau known as KFVS. It was the first station in Southeast Missouri and Southern Illinois. They had a very small brick building located on south Frederick Street, not far from Grandpa's home. They stirred Grandpa's imagination and made supplies, such as crystals, wire, headset earphones, and other needs of amateurs. Grandpa had a friend who was a radio bug.

The first crystal set that Grandpa ever built was very simple. It consisted of a small crystal, a coil of wire and a set of earphones. A copper wire was bent into the shape of a small arm and was moved to different spots on the crystal to tune in different frequencies. Earphones were fastened to the coil, and it would transmit the sound to the earphones. It required skill, patience, and intent listening to find the few stations it would pick up.

Reception was very limited. KFVS, the local station, came in clear when it was on the air. Several other stations were received if conditions were right and you had the patience to find them. (It wasn't as easy as turning a dial on a present day radio or TV). WLW in Cincinnati was a strong signal in those early days and could usually be tuned in during the evenings and at nights. WGN was

Grandpa's favorite station, and like WLW you could usually get it at night.

Grandpa loved big bands, and Guy Lombardo and
Wayne King were holding sway at the Argon and Trianon
Ball Rooms in Chicago and usually had a radio broadcast
nightly. He would listen late at night in order to hear all the
big bands possible. Grandpa also build some of the first
battery powered tube radios in his area. Grandpa says,
"These early experiences with crystal sets and home-built
radios brought a life-time love for radio and television
broadcasting.

Another institution that played an important role in the
formative years of Grandpa's childhood was the Sunday
School. Grandpa had a Sunday School teacher who was
over six feet tall, very lean and bald-headed. His initials
were L.L., and the boys all called him "Long Legs." All the
boys in the class were full of "old nick" and a constant irri-
tation to L.L. They wore his patience thin. One Sunday
morning the boys were especially trying, and they caused
him to lose his temper and say some things he later regretted. The next Sunday he came into the class and with tears
flowing down his face said, "I am sorry, I lost my temper."
Grandpa realized that it was not L.L. who should be apolo-
gizing, but it was Grandpa and all the boys in the class who
had provoked him to anger. That Sunday when L.L. said, "I
am sorry," he taught his greatest lesson, Grandpa knew that
it takes a big man to apologize under any condition, and
that it is especially difficult when someone else is at fault.
Grandpa says, "I cannot remember any other lesson L.L.
taught, but I will always remember the lesson we learned."

The Maple Avenue Sunday School had a basketball
team and belonged to a Sunday School league composed of
Lutherans, First Baptist, Res Star Baptist, Grace Methodist,
First Methodist, Evangelical and Presbyterians. Grandpa

played on the Maple Avenue Methodist team and spent many happy hours practicing and playing while in grade and high school. The Sunday School League helped keep him off the street and out of trouble.

Bible stories, hymns, and gospel songs were an important part of Grandpa's training. Grandpa says, "They have shaped and motivated my life." Grandpa loved to let his imagination run wild while reading the story of David and Goliath. He liked David because he was a simple shepherd boy, loved music, and most importantly he had faith to believe that God was active in his daily life. God did not sit somewhere above and far away from life, but He participated in it at all times. As a small boy in his imagination, Grandpa would put himself in David's place. He imagined that he was the one who cast off the King's armor, carefully selecting the stones for the sling, and then went out and defeated the Philistine giant. Step by step he played the role and walked where David walked.

Grandpa has used this lesson throughout his life. He has found that any time a person sets out to do something worthwhile, there is always a Goliath, sometimes a whole committee, that will challenge what you are trying to do. When this happened subconsciously, Grandpa would go through this imaginary process with David. Grandpa says, "What often looked like sure defeat would turn into a triumphant victory."

Grandpa learned a valuable lesson. God is always available to help us in times of need if we are willing to place our time, talents, and skills in his hands, and let him use them. God takes us just as we are, with what we have, and accomplishes the things that need to be done.

From the earliest days of his life, Grandpa remembers singing such old hymns as "Jesus Loves Me," "Jesus Loves the Little Children," "The Old Rugged Cross," "Rock of

Ages," and many others. Grandpa says, "These songs have brought a heap of blessings to my life. I simply bow before God and say 'Thank You' to the many hymn and gospel song writers who were inspired to write them."

Year twelve was a time of transition from childhood to the teens. Grandpa started to high school, and a lot of adjustments were necessary. In many ways, he grew up very quickly, in other ways he remained a child. It was a difficult period. Grandpa says, "There were a number of factors that helped me make the transition without serious problems."

Grandpa joined the Boy Scouts shortly after his 12th birthday. He loved scoutmaster Bob, who greatly influenced his life. Grandpa liked to work on the requirements that led to becoming a First Class Scout. He loved the games and activities with the other scouts in Troop 9. Grandpa spent many hours learning to tie different kinds of knots, like the half hitch, the bowline, and many others. He learned how to build a fire without matches and many other tactics for survival. He enjoyed studying about first aid, and learned many practical and usable things. He earned a number of Merit Badges.

Scout Camp was really fun. Camp Rotary was located near Grasse, MO, on Castor River where there was swimming, fishing, and plenty of woods for hiking. It was here Grandpa also learned leaf and tree identification.

All the guys kept talking about how much fun it was to hunt snipes. The third night about 10:00 p.m., they took Grandpa into the woods and found a deep hollow. Since it was Grandpa's first hunt, they all agreed to let him stand in the hollow and hold the big brown burlap bag. Grandpa was to be as quiet as possible and hold the mouth of the bag wide open next to the ground. One of the boys said, "We will go up to the top of the hill and spread out in all different directions and beat the bushes. That will cause the snipes to run down into the hollow and into the bag."

Plans were made for all of them to meet at Grandpa's location at midnight. All of it sounded very logical to Grandpa. He heard the boys scampering up the hill through the woods. Finally, he could no longer hear them. It was very still and dark, and there were many strange sounds. Grandpa began to feel that things were not quite right. The longer he waited, the more frightened he became. He kept looking at his watch. Finally midnight arrived, and there was no trace of the boys. Grandpa could not hear a sound, and it slowly and surely dawned on him that he was alone deep in the woods after midnight "holding the bag." Grandpa had been deceived by his so-called friends. He was nearly paralyzed by fear, but he made a decision and started running as hard as his legs would carry him. Grandpa could not find his way back to the camp. He began to think. The camp was to the east of where the boys had left him. He located the North Star, and he knew the moon was to the east. He headed to the east and finally came to a road that he recognized as the road that ran from the highway to the camp. He turned to his right and passed the home of the caretaker of the camp. It was only a matter of minutes until he was approaching the camp.

At about 1:30 a.m. a tired and weary twelve year old boy, who was very angry, arrived at the camp. All the lights were out, and every boy in the bunkhouse seemed to be asleep. However, when a weary Grandpa finally crawled into the bunk, he heard them giggling.

He decided not to mention the incident the next morning, and at breakfast it was not mentioned. By 10:00 a.m., some of the boys could no longer stand the silence and asked Grandpa how he liked snipe hunting? Grandpa smiled and said, "I really had fun and I can't wait to teach some other boy who has never had the experience of snipe hunting." It was never mentioned again. Grandpa said, "I learned an important lesson. Even your friends will leave you holding the bag if you are gullible."

Scoutmaster Bob was in a boat with several scouts. The boys were clowning around, jumping in and out of the boat. Several times they almost turned it over. The Scoutmaster was in the back of the boat with his old pipe in his mouth. (His only bad habit). He had on an old dilapidated hat pulled down over his face to protect him from the sun. He warned the boys to be careful and said, "Remember, I can't swim." About that time the boat tipped over. All of them were dumped into the water. When Bob came up his pipe was still in his mouth, his old hat was floating. It was apparent from the look on his face he was in trouble. He went under again and came back up. Grandpa and another boy went into action and dived in and grabbed him. They pulled him up on the bank. After several minutes of coughing and spitting out water, he gasped for breath and soon was breathing normally. He looked at the boys and simply said, "Thanks!" A bunch of scared boys breathed a sigh of relief. They had almost drowned the man they most admired. Grandpa says, "I hope we all learned a lesson. Life is too sacred to take chances."

Grandpa says, "An old Model T Ford with a brass radiator was very rare, even when I was 12 years old." Grandpa had a friend whose father was the proud owner of such a vehicle. Grandpa's friend enticed his father to let him and Grandpa drive to Castor River near the scout camp for a three day fishing trip. After much persuasion, Grandpa's parents agreed to let him go. The old Model "T" had one little problem, the radiator had a slow leak, and they would have to stop to fill it up. The boys arrived safely and set up their "pup" tents in which they would later sleep. They spent the rest of the day fishing off the banks with a pole and line. They caught several nice keepers which they cooked for supper over an open fire.

A unique experience awaited the boys. The next day they met and made friends with a lawyer from their home town. He had a boat and was fishing with trot lines, and he invited them to help him bait the lines. Late that day, he told them it was necessary for him to return home that afternoon for business reasons and that he would return the following day. He told the boys they could use the boat and run lines that evening and in the morning. The boys were elated.

That afternoon they ran the lines and caught a number of nice sized fish. They baited the lines for overnight. The next morning they ran the lines. Grandpa was taking fish off the line and baiting the hooks, and his friend was rowing the boat. One of the lines seemed to be hung and Grandpa could hardly pull it up to the surface. When Grandpa finally got to where he thought the line was hung, he could hardly believe his eyes. He yelled, "Wow! Ernie, we have a fish on this line as big as I am. I can't get it over the side of the boat." His friend quickly came to help, and the two boys tugged and pulled until they rolled the huge catfish over the side of the boat.

The boys immediately headed for camp. They decided that no one would believe their story unless they saw the fish. Grandpa and his friends made a decision to take the fish home alive. They soaked several burlap bags with water and wrapped them around the fish. They left immediately to drive the 40 miles back home in the old Model "T." It was necessary to stop at every branch to wet down the fish and to fill the radiator of the car. Four and a half hours later, they arrived at home with the catfish still alive.

The boys posed for a picture with the fish tied to a pole that rested on each of their shoulders with the fish hanging between them. The tail of the fish touched the ground, and it weighed in at 25 pounds. The picture and a story of their remarkable experience made the local newspaper. The story was now and forever verifiable (quite a fish story and hard to believe). Grandpa says, "It is the truth." Note the following:

It is the largest fish Grandpa ever caught

It was caught on a borrowed line.

It was caught in a borrowed boat.

It made fishing a life-time habit with Grandpa.

This is the stuff that keeps Grandpa ticking. No book could fully contain the many wonders of Grandpa's childhood. These wonders continue to motivate Grandpa's life today since the recollection of them is as "real" as the experience itself was then.

Grandpa says, "Today we are constantly bombarded by the media, TV, and movie industry with stories of abused children, youth, and even adults, who blame all their behavioral problems on the treatment they received during their childhood." Grandpa believes that in so doing, they avoid responsibility for their own actions.

Grandpa says, "I can never remember a single experience when I felt I was abused or neglected by my parents. I did not feel sibling rivalry between myself, my brother, or my sister."

Grandpa continues, "I bow in humble adoration before the God of grace and pay the highest tribute to my parents, who gave me my remarkable childhood. It is an awesome wonder! I did not choose my parents, they were gifts of God's marvelous grace."

This is the important stuff from which Grandpa's life has been shaped and motivated.

CHAPTER 3
A CHARMED CIRCLE

Grandpa says, "The best way to describe the family in which l was raised is found in the following three words, 'A Charmed Circle.'" Grandpa says, "We had faith, fun, respect for one another, and above all, our lives had meaning and purpose. We lived each day."

Charm, as used in describing Grandpa's family, does not mean some magical power to ward off evil. It does mean there is something attractive and fascinating about this family group made up of ordinary people, who had faults, failures, and troubles common to all families. Grandpa says, "The thing that gave charm to my family was an awareness of God's presence at work in the center of the lives of every member of the group, bringing forgiveness for our sins, strength for our weakness, healing for our hurts, and comfort for our sorrows."

Any group of ordinary people forming a family can become aware of God's presence at work in their daily lives. When they do so, they will become both attractive and fascinating.

If you really want to know "What Makes Grandpa Tick?" you must know something about this family, beginning with his father. Grandpa's dad was a farm boy who grew up on a farm in Cape County, about eight miles north and west of Cape Girardeau, Missouri. His father owned a small farm that adjoined the old McKendree Chapel (the oldest Methodist Church west of the Mississippi River). Grandpa's dad moved to the city and became a carpenter by trade. He was very proud of the many quality homes he built. He was a good provider for his family and was a model of integrity. Grandpa's dad added common sense, stability, and practicality to the life of the family. His favorite poem was, "The House by the Side of the Road." He loved all kinds of people and tried to live out the truth of this poem daily.

Grandpa's mom was the spiritual leader of the tribe and loved her family and freely expressed her affection openly to every member. Grandpa's mom was a writer who had a number of her meditations and poems published in The Upper Room, and the W. S.C. S. paper of the Methodist Church. Grandpa says, "My mom was always deeply involved in the daily activities of us children." She was a good housekeeper who always provided good meals and plenty of snacks in-between for the kids.

Grandpa's Grandfather B, his maternal grandfather, lived with the family during most of Grandpa's childhood and teen years, until the time of his death. His favorite pastime was reading as he sat in his high backed rocking chair. He loved his grandchildren including Grandpa, and did his best to spoil them. Grandfather B's trademark was a brown corduroy coat with huge pockets that stamped an unforgettable image in Grandpa's mind. All the grandchildren were fascinated by those pockets that he always kept filled with all kinds of treats such as Juicy Fruit chewing gum, bubble gum, lemon drops, peppermint sticks, Hershey bars, pennies, and the list went on and on. Grandfather B was a good example for his grand-kids. He only had two bad habits. He chewed Star tobacco and smoked Virginia Cheroot cigars. The only word of slang he ever used was, "Dad burn it."

(surely God must have smiled when he heard this dear old man get aggravated and say, "Dad burn it.")

Grandpa says, "Grandfather B added a rare sense of character and charm to the family circle that helped enrich the lives of us grand-kids. I have always loved the rocking chair, and I am sure it was Grandfather B who planted the seed. It is no accident that on the cover of this book is a rocking chair."

Little Sister was the oldest living child in Grandpa's childhood family. She was very small in stature but blessed with a brain that made her outstanding in spite of a physical handicap. Grandpa always thought of her as his little sister because of her size, even though she was three years older. Grandpa's little sister was an excellent musician who started taking piano lessons when she was in about the fourth or fifth grade in school. She served as the pianist for her church for years. When the church purchased an organ she took lessons and became an excellent organist. She served as organist at the Maple Avenue Methodist Church in Cape Girardeau, Missouri, for many years. She brought happiness and joy to the family through her musical talents. Little Sister also taught a Sunday School class for many years. Grandpa's little sister was a straight "A" student and had an excellent mind, winning the State of Missouri High School typing contest in her senior year. This provided her with a scholarship at a business college. Following graduation from the business college, she was employed by the Missouri Utilities Company where she remained many years, until retirement. She received many promotions in the company (It had merged with the Union Electric of St. Louis) and became the first woman Executive Officer in the company's history. Grandpa says, "I am very proud of my sister and the things she accomplished. It is a distinct privilege to call her my 'Little Sister.'" On

December 22, 1996, an angel from God completed her mission. Grandpa says, "Her mission was to enrich the life of our family through her music, her brilliant mind, her courage to overcome her handicap, her love and generosity. She effectively accomplished that mission and returned to God from whence she came. She was my 'Little Sister' who continues to influence and shape my life. Little Sister is one of the reasons l am still ticking."

Grandpa's kid brother loved to sing like the rest of the family and even more. In later years of his life, he became a singing witness for Jesus. Grandpa says, "Most of us are worrying witnesses and accomplish little. He was a singing witness who won others to Christ. Kid Brother sang in lay witness missions throughout the mid west. Grandpa's kid brother got up singing and was still singing when he went to bed at night. Like Grandpa's dad, kid brother was a building contractor who loved to build good homes. Grandpa says, "I am proud to call him my 'Kid Brother.' He helped motivate and bring joy to my life."

Grandpa completed the family circle, composed of six strong-willed individuals who often disagreed on everything from politics to sports. Sometimes arguments would be loud and long. Grandpa was fascinated by the differences of each member of the family. They looked different, talked different, thought different, and dressed different. Kid Brother liked mashed potatoes, and Grandpa liked plain old boiled potatoes (their mom often fixed both kinds at the same meal to please them). With all their differences, the bond of faith and love made them compatible (God surely must have laughed at some of their silly arguments. What a big job he had with this bunch on his hands). He must have laughed out loud and said, "I sure made them different."

Grandpa says, "The one thing I remember most about my mom and dad was that they were always there when any one of us kids needed them." When Grandpa would get home from school and open the door and yell, "Mom," she was there. When Grandpa had a problem, he went to his dad. He was there. Grandpa says, "This brought a sense of security that has remained with me to this day."

Grandpa's dad bought a new 1923 Model T Ford. It was one of the first cars in the south end of town where the family lived. A lot of fun revolved around this car. The family looked forward to the Sunday afternoon drives to many new and interesting places in the surrounding area.

Grandpa's dad drove the family to Cape Rock Park where they learned how Cape Girardeau got its name. Two and a half centuries ago, a young French Marine Ensign by the name of Jean Baptiste Girardot (Girardeau) established a trading post on a high rock ledge that projected into the waters of the mighty Mississippi River. The river, in striking the base of this ledge, made a cove or "cape." It gave this French soldier an extensive view and shelter for his boats.

The name on early maps was spelled, "Cape Girardot," "Cape Girardo," "Cape Girardeau," and thus, the site became known to early voyagers as "Cape Girardeau," an obvious modification of "Girardot." This is the only inland "cape" in the world. This early French trading post is now what is known as Cape Rock park. It is north of the city of Cape Girardeau.

One of Grandpa's favorite parks to visit on a Sunday afternoon was the site of the "Trail of Tears." The family would all jump into the old Model T and would drive ten miles north of Cape Girardeau to a place on the banks of the Mississippi where during the winter of 1838-39, 13,000 Cherokee Indians were exiled from their homeland in the east by the federal treaty and forced to march to a desolate

Indian reservation in Oklahoma. The 800 mile march took its toll on the proud Cherokees. One of every four Indians died during the winter they spent near the Mississippi River. Grandpa says, "I stood there as a boy and wept when I thought of the suffering, hunger, sickness and death that was wrought on these Indians by we Americans who call our country a nation of justice and freedom."

Grandpa's dad was doing much more than taking his family on enjoyable Sunday afternoon rides in the Model T, he was teaching them history and truth about the sacredness of human personality. The lessons were unforgettable and still motivate Grandpa at 80 years of age.

Grandpa's hometown is called the "City of Roses on the River." One of Grandpa's favorite drives was the ten mile stretch from Cape to Jackson. In 1931, the "Ten Mile Garden" was planted. Twenty thousand rose bushes were planted along old Highway 61.

Red roses were planted on one side, and white roses on the other. These colors represented the North and South of the Civil War. Hundreds of evergreen trees formed a background against the great native trees and created a panorama of breathtaking beauty. In 1931, Harry O'Brien, Roving Editor for "Better Homes and Gardens," wrote, "There is nothing of the kind to equal it in the United States." Much to Grandpa's regret, this beautiful "Ten Mile Garden" was a victim of progress when a new highway and freeway were built.

Cape Girardeau, the place where Grandpa was born and grew up, had a great influence in shaping his life.

Grandpa's dad built snow sleds for his kids. They had wooden runners covered with a strip of metal on the bottom of each runner to make them slide more effectively and so they would not wear out so quickly. When a winter storm would cover the ground with snow, Grandpa's dad would tie ropes from each one of their sleds and to the back of the Model T and pull them through the neighborhood streets. Sometimes as many as six or eight kids from the neighborhood would hang on with their sleds. This was great sport that all the family enjoyed. Grandpa's mom would ride in the car and have as much fun as the rest of the family. Grandpa says, "Parents involved in their children's daily activities, including fun, make a major difference in the lives of their children."

Grandpa's dad and mom and all the kids decorated a very beautiful tree before Christmas. Grandpa did a very stupid thing the next day. He and a neighbor boy got into an argument about whether cotton would burn. The friend knew it would, but Grandpa said it wouldn't. In order to prove his point, Grandpa lit a match and touched it to the cotton skirting under the Christmas tree. The cotton ignited instantly and caught the tree on fire. Grandpa's mom happened to come into the room just as it happened. She grabbed the tree and with the help of the boys, pulled it out on the porch and then into the yard. This prevented the house from catching on fire. Grandpa's mom and each of the boys had minor burns on their hands. The tree and all the decorations were completely destroyed. A major tragedy was barely escaped. Grandpa and his mom both cried. Grandpa felt miserable.

Late that afternoon when Grandpa's dad came home, they decided there would be no tree that Christmas. Grandpa was devastated because he had ruined Christmas for all the other members of the family. The next day Grandpa's dad was gone for several hours. When he came home he was carrying another tree that he had cut. Grandpa's mom managed to come up with enough homemade ornaments and trimming to decorate the tree. All the family was pleasantly surprised, including Grandpa.

Grandpa's dad gathered the kids around and explained that he and Grandpa's mom had talked last night and reversed their previous decision. Grandpa's dad said "Christmas is a time of joy and celebration regardless of the circumstances." He also explained that Grandpa would be disciplined after the first of the year Grandpa would be grounded for two months with a number of privileges being withdrawn. Grandpa was both pleased and sorry. He felt forgiven, and though the punishment seemed severe, he thought it was fair. He knew he deserved to be punished. Grandpa was glad this would not rob Little Sister and Kid Brother of their Christmas. One thing for sure, he never wanted to do anything that stupid again. Grandpa says, "God must have shook his head and wondered if he ever made anyone that stupid."

Christmas morning Grandpa and all the family were up early and gathered around the tree. They enjoyed their gifts, and it was a wonderful day. Grandpa's heart was filled with gratitude as they sat down together and his dad thanked God for the abundant food that graced their table, for one another, and for the greatest gift of all, God's gift of His Son, Jesus. They laughed and enjoyed the delicious food Grandpa's mom had prepared. That evening they gathered around Little Sister seated at the piano and sang "Joy to the World" and "Silent Night." Grandpa says, "I felt tears roll down my cheeks as I thought of the near tragedy I had caused, I hugged my old dog, Teddy, and was grateful the family was not missing all these wonderful things. I was glad to be a member of a family where there was forgiveness, a second chance, love and acceptance (God surely smiled)." Grandpa has forgotten the gifts he received that Christmas, but he has never forgotten the spirit of his loving family. Grandpa says, "This is why I call my family a 'Charmed Circle.' It is the real stuff of which my life is made. Tick! Tock!"

One of the most graphic scenes that Grandpa remembers from his childhood is the following: Little Sister is on her piano bench; Grandpa's dad is seated in his favorite chair; Grandfather B is in his high-backed rocker; and the rest of the family is gathered about the piano. Grandpa loved this time of singing together. Grandpa's Little Sister had hundreds of pieces of popular sheet music, a number of hymnals, and a number of traditional song books. Grandpa says, "Singing was a regular ritual in our family." The family would sing such songs as "In a Little Spanish Town," "Charmaine," "Carolina Moon," "Blue Heaven," "Star Dust," "Girl of My Dreams," "Good Night Sweetheart," and the list could go on. After singing popular songs for twenty or thirty minutes, the family would sing hymns, "What a Friend We Have in Jesus," "The Old Rugged Cross," and many others. Sometimes Grandpa or Kid Brother would sing one verse as a solo as others hummed in the background. Grandpa says, "This brought us together as a strong family unit through the power of music. This is family life at its best and is the stuff of my live."

St. Louis was about 125 miles north of Cape Girardeau. It was a real treat to visit the nearest large metropolitan area with its many parks and interesting sights. Grandpa's dad would drive them to Shaw's Garden, old Sportsman's Park, where the St. Louis Brown's and Cardinal's used to play ball. Of course, they always visited the Forest Park Zoo, which was one of their favorite spots.

Grandpa says, "The zoo was a fantastic and exciting place for kids. This was my family's favorite place to visit." The lions and tigers gave stellar performances several times a day. The trained elephants were really a joy to watch. The monkey show was a scream and delighted the whole family. The gorillas and baboons were frightening and were watched with care. The huge glass enclosures for the birds of every size, shape and color were a land of fantasy.

Late one afternoon, Grandpa, his dad, and Kid Brother decided they wanted to visit the Highlands, which was a large amusement park across the highway and to the south of the zoo. Grandpa's mom and Little Sister remained at the zoo watching the zebras.

The amusement park was filled with hundreds of people, and all seemed to be having a great time. As Grandpa's Dad, Kid Brother, and Grandpa walked down the midway, they came to a place called the Fun House. People on the inside were laughing and screaming and having a ball. Grandpa wanted to go through the Fun House. His Dad declined, but quickly purchased tickets for Grandpa and Kid Brother. Kid Brother was scared and refused to go. Grandpa was scared too but wasn't about to let them know he was afraid, and so he entered the Fun House alone. He made his way down a narrow dark passage that opened into a dimly lighted room with mirrors that distorted the way a person looked. Grandpa says, "I looked at one mirror and I was very wide and fat; another, and I was very tall and thin. Another mirror made me look so grotesque it frightened me even worse. I was really uncomfortable and shook-up. Fear began to grip my emotions. I went down another dark, narrow passageway where it was too dark to even see my own hand. Suddenly I walked over a louvered opening in the floor, and air rushed up into my face. I nearly stopped breathing. I gritted my teeth and moved on saying to myself, 'I won't be afraid.' I stepped on a board that worked like a see-saw, and it threw me up against the wall at the end of the passage. Fear gripped my heart, and it pounded against the walls of my chest. It seemed like I had a thousand pounds sitting in the middle of my chest. I was paralyzed by fear and could not move. Tears flowed freely down my cheeks, and I cried out, 'Dad!' over and over again! Time seemed to stand still as I stood there and cried."

"I heard an insistent voice above, saying, 'Look up sonny! Look up!' The voice was so commanding that I finally looked up, and there was a carnival roustabout on a catwalk above the passageway. He had a small flashlight shinning down into the darkness. He kept saying, 'Look up sonny! Look up! Look up sonny! Listen to me! Listen to me! Keep looking up and follow the light. I will soon lead you outside to your father.' I quit sobbing and looked up. I kept looking up and following the light. I soon broke out into the sunlight, and there was my Dad. I jumped into his waiting arms. Peace and security flooded my boyish heart, all my fear was gone, and I knew I was safe."

Grandpa says, "I learned a most important lesson about fear and life. What made the difference? My father's arms! My father's love! I learned a very important truth, God's presence is with us, and underneath are His everlasting arms when the dark places seem to overcome us in life." Life has its dark place where we cannot see the way, but God has given us a light that shines into the darkness. He has given us the "Light of the World." His name is Jesus, and we find grace, love, and security as we look up to him in prayer and follow the light. All the darkness in the world cannot put out that light. Grandpa says, "I have told this story at many funerals and beside the beds of the sick and dying to give comfort and hope to people in their darkest experiences. This experience has been a great source of comfort and strength to me in my hours of testing."

A fun place in Grandpa's childhood home was the table around which the family gathered to share with one another what was happening in their daily lives. Sometimes they shared a joke, a lesson learned, or a new-found friend.

The table was a great place to communicate with one another. No subject was off limits. Spoken grace was always the first item on the agenda at every meal. Giving "Thanks to God" was as much a part of Grandpa's childhood family life as breathing.

Grandpa says, "I can never remember a meal during my childhood at which the family did not pause to thank God for the food on our table, and the many blessings we received daily."

Table grace was a shared experience, and each one took his or her turn expressing the spoken grace. One time when Grandpa was very young, he was expressing the words of thanks. That day they were having his favorite meal, small chunks of ham cut in navy beans. Grandpa was extremely hungry and got in a hurry. He said, "Bless this food dear Heavenly Father, please pass me the beans!" Every member of the family broke out in laughter (Grandpa looks back on that scene and thinks God joined in the laughter). God surely said, "At least he took time to thank me, and he is learning a valuable lesson." There were many fun times at the table in Grandpa's childhood home.

Grandpa says, "Table grace is a great teacher that provides a common center of communications where members can touch base with one another daily." A little boy was heard to say, "Our family doesn't need a home, all we need is a garage. We are on the go all the time." Grandpa says, "Grace slows us down and gives us time to catch our spiritual breath." Grace is essential in our tense and hurried world.

Grandpa says, "A real family learns very quickly it is difficult to be angry with another member of the family when they sit down together and pray at the same table. Grace restores broken relationships." Table grace teaches people that they do not pray because they are perfect, but they pray because of the imperfections that divide them. Grandpa says, "We do not pray because we feel like it. We pray because God loves us in spite of our sins and regardless of how we feel. He continues to bestow His goodness and grace on our lives even when we are bad, and when we are not even aware of His presence. Table grace helps us to be aware of the talents and strengths of one another." Grandpa's mom started this tradition in his family because she knew it was a sure way to keep the whole family aware of God's presence at work in their daily lives. Grandpa says, "God gave the grace, forgiveness, patience, and understanding that made my family of six ordinary people into a 'Charmed Circle.'"

Grandpa says, "I vividly remember the walls of my childhood home. The walls in each room had their own unique teaching. Walls do talk."

On the walls in Grandpa's childhood home hung a painting of an elderly man with hands folded as he gives thanks to God for daily bread. A loaf of unbroken bread and a bowl of soup are before him on the table. Alongside the bread is a Holy Bible, and the man's glasses are folded on top. Grandpa says, "This is one of my favorite paintings, and a picture of it is etched in my mind. My wife and I have the same painting over our table now, and have had it there for many years." The painting recognizes the presence of God working in the home, and is a reminder that God is the source of all blessings. The walls of a home can speak loud and clear about what is really important in life to those who live there.

A little plaque hung on one of the walls of the living room in Grandpa's childhood home. It clearly and plainly stated, "Prayer changes things." Grandpa says, "What a tremendous statement, and I knew it was true because I had seen prayer change things in my own home." It took

Grandpa many years to understand how prayer changes things. Grandpa says, "After many years I began to comprehend how prayer changes things. It first changes the people who pray. When people change, they change things. That is why prayer is so essential to good living." Prayer is a person's connecting link to God. Grandpa says, "Through prayer I receive forgiveness for my sins, healing for my hurts, and wholeness for my fragmented life." Blessed is the home where the walls speak loud and clear of the necessity of prayer.

Each bedroom had its own particular teaching. In one room which Grandpa shared with Kid Brother, there was a painting of a small boy kneeling by his bedside with folded hands and uplifted eyes. Grandpa would look at it and think, "Prayer is for a kid like me, not just for adults." Grandpa says, "I did not always pray, but I was always aware that I should and that it was very important."

Grandpa says, "Without any reservation, I recommend family religion as a 'cure all' for the ills of modern family life. The home is the best place to teach faith, and the walls are a video screen to help us. It is a free visual aid." Someone has said, "A picture is worth a thousand words."

Grandpa says, "My mom made sure there was always something good to read. The Holy Bible and The Upper Room devotional were always visible and available. The Holy Bible was usually open to a highlighted scripture for the day. One could not live in my childhood home and ignore the Holy Bible. It was always visible."

The Upper Room was important to all of Grandpa's family and helped each member to think about the suggested scripture for the day and to understand what someone else thought about that particular verse.

Grandpa says, "My dad enriched all of our lives by the stories he told about his youth and his early married life.

His stories were interesting and funny." The following is a tale Grandpa loved to hear his dad tell. Grandpa's dad and several other boys watched the traveling preacher drive his buggy up to the church one Sunday evening. The ground was covered with ice and snow, and it was very slick. During the service, the boys filled the back of the buggy with large rocks. After the service was over, the preacher started home. As he started up a steep grade, the horse's hooves slipped, causing the horse to nearly fall. It could not pull the buggy up the hill. The preacher fussed and fumed. The boys were hiding in the woods nearby and could not contain their laughter. The preacher found the rocks in the back of the buggy and unloaded them, fussing all the while about those aggravating boys. After unloading the rocks, he got back into the buggy and was able to continue over the hill on his journey toward home. The fun was over.

One story Grandpa's dad told left a lasting impression on Grandpa. When Grandpa's dad first moved to town from the farm, he had no trained skill and he got a job digging a ditch. About noon he made a decision that would affect the rest of his life. Grandpa's dad crawled out of the ditch and quit the job. One of the other men asked him what he was going to do. He said, "I am going to get a job as a carpenter. The man he asked for a job liked him and gave him a job. The man stood watching him as he went to work and asked, "Young man, how long have you been a carpenter?" Grandpa's dad replied, "For about five minutes, and I plan to be the best carpenter you ever hired. I plan to be a carpenter the rest of my life." The man appreciated his grit and determination and kept him until he became an excellent carpenter and builder. Grandpa's dad went on to built a successful career as a building contractor and businessman.

Grandpa's favorite story that his dad told was a story about his faith. When Grandpa's dad and mom had been married for about three years, they had little money and their first child was very sick. The doctor had called in the home and given them a prescription, and they had no money to pay for it. Even though he did not know how he was going to pay for the prescription, Grandpa's dad headed for the drug store. As he walked along, he talked to God and told him he had done all he could do and that he needed help. Grandpa's dad looked down, and there in his path was a large shining silver dollar. That was the exact cost of the prescription. Grandpa's dad said, "Most people would say that it was a coincidence, but I think it was an answer to prayer." Grandpa says, "You can call it what you like, but I agree with my dad. It was an answer to a prayer."

Grandpa says, "I could fill two books with the many miracles of God's amazing grace and goodness that have been evident in my family. A charmed circle creates the substance of my life. Families are forever."

Grandpa says, "I did not choose to be born into my family, being born into my family was a gift of God's grace."

Grandpa says, "Fun is a balance wheel of life that keeps us from taking ourselves too seriously."

CHAPTER 4
FOCUS ON FUN

Grandpa and five other boys walked from their homes on South Pacific Street to Central High School. It was their first day of high school. Two of the five boys were 13 years of age, two were 14, and one was 15. Grandpa was only 12. All through his high school career, he competed and associated with peers who were two and three years older. He thought this was great, but it had many disadvantages.

Old Central High School was located on Pacific Street, one mile north of his home on the same street and in the center of the city. The boys were having a lot of fun kidding each other and picking on three girls walking in front of them. It was a wonderful day. When they arrived at the school, there were several hundred students milling around the yard and in the halls. The air was filled with excitement, and everyone seemed to be having a ball. Grandpa did not know most of them and as he took it all in, he decided this was really going to be a fun four years. He met many new students that were to become life long friends.

At the registration desk a senior, by the name of John, was assigned to be Grandpa's big brother for the first week of school. John showed Grandpa to his homeroom and introduced him to his homeroom teacher. Miss Eileen and Grandpa became good friends. She was pretty, intelligent, and made Grandpa feel at ease. Throughout the day, John showed him to the rooms where each class met. There was a different teacher and a room for each subject. Grandpa liked this because it broke the monotony of the day and gave the students a chance to have a little fun in-between classes.

Grandpa says, "I made a decision that during the next four years, I would focus on fun." This, of course, would lead to some problems. Grandpa had a good mind and was capable of making all "A's." With the focus on fun, he settled for "B's," and this troubled some of his teachers who knew he was capable of doing much better. Grandpa says, "Drama, ballroom dancing, and big bands captured my attention and provided outlets for good clean fun during my four years of high school."

One of Grandpa's English teachers convinced him that he should join the Drama Club. He was a ham to begin with, and he really enjoyed the short plays they produced in the classroom. Later, during his sophomore year, Grandpa was chosen for a part in the high school play, and it was open to the general public for two nights and to the student body on Friday afternoon.

The play was based on the book, Penrod, and Grandpa was given the part of a little tongue-tied black boy, named Vermon. Vermon and his brother, Hermon, were friends of Penrod and members of his gang. Two of Grandpa's close friends played the parts of Hermon and Penrod.

Grandpa says, "This play was one of the highlights of my high school days. I really enjoyed the play and the fellowship of other members of the cast. It provided fun for many months to come."

"Penrod" had a sister who was being courted by a man named, Dade, who was planning to marry her. He was a natural enemy of Penrod and his friends, and they were convinced they had to protect Penrod's sister from this villain. They would spy on "Ole Dade" as they called him, when he came to see Penrod's sister. Vermon was given the dangerous task of hiding behind furniture on the verandah and in other out-of-the-way places to watch the activities of the couple. He would then report to Penrod and the rest of the gang. Vermon could not pronounce an "S." On a number of occasions, he would cry out to the others, "I tree him! I tree him! I tree ole Mista Dade!" This line became a badge of distinction for Grandpa. It made Grandpa the star of the show and follows him even to this day. It provided many hilarious occasions all through his high school days. In crucial moments at just the right time, Grandpa would cry out, "I tree him, I tree him" and it always was good for a laugh.

One evening Grandpa and several friends were sitting in the balcony of the Broadway Theater watching an exciting Tom Mix Western. Tom Mix was being followed by an Indian who was trying to kill him. Mix was crouched behind a large boulder for protection. Unbeknown to him, the Indian was creeping up behind him over the top of the boulder with a knife in his hand, poised and ready to plunge the knife into the heart of Mix. Everyone in the theater had their eyes riveted on the screen, no one moved, and the silence was deadening. Suddenly a voice broke the silence when a desperate cry came from the balcony, "I tree him! I tree him! I tree that old Indian!" The theater went wild with laughter and applause as Grandpa stole the climatic moment of the movie, ruining its effect. Most people knew it was Grandpa. It took several minutes to get the place quieted down. The next day Grandpa was called into the principal's office where he was lectured about education being much more important than having fun, and "showing off." Before Grandpa left the office the principal smiled and said, "I admit I broke up with laughter when you cried out. Your timing was perfect." Grandpa felt good as he left the office and he thought to himself, the principal was right about the importance of education. However, it is likewise true, that we need to laugh. Fun is a balance wheel in a world of tension and trouble, it is necessary to make life whole. Grandpa says, "God must like to have a good time because he made fun a part of life." The problem is knowing when to have fun and when to be serious. Grandpa confesses that he often erred on the side of fun during those days. Grandpa says, "Balance is everything in building the good life."

At 80, Grandpa still has a few friends who are still living and remember that evening in the Broadway Theater.

Grandpa started to high school in 1929, the year of the great depression, and its effects were evident in the lives of people everywhere. Most families were struggling financially, even the wealthy, and there was much stress and unhappiness. Thinking back, Grandpa felt the need for levity in the lives of most people was never greater.

Ballroom dancing and Big Bands were at the epitome of popularity, and Grandpa was a great fan of both. These were both good clean outlets for Grandpa with his focus on fun.

Katie was a girl in her junior year in high school who met Grandpa during the first few weeks of Grandpa's freshman year. Katie sort of adopted him as a younger brother that first year. She loved to dance and knew all the latest dance steps and taught them to Grandpa. They loved to dance together, and their relationship lasted through her senior year and even while she was a student at Southeast Missouri State College. They were never romantically involved, but were simply good friends who loved to dance.

There were many ballrooms and dance halls in Cape Girardeau, including the Marquette Hotel, Idanha Hotel, the Armory, the Community Building at the Park, and a Roller Skate Rink where dancing was held every Saturday night. Occasionally, a Big Band was scheduled at the Houck

Field House, of the Southeast Missouri State University, including Henry Bussi, Guy Lombardo, Wayne King, and others. Grandpa attended dances in all these places. Grandpa also had friends who were members of the Cape Country Club where many dances for high school and college age kids were held. He was invited to many of these and enjoyed them all.

Cape Girardeau was on the Mississippi River between St. Louis, Missouri, and Memphis, Tennessee. Both cities were nationally known for their contributions to the musical tradition known as the Blues and Dixie Land Jazz. Cape Girardeau was the home of a number of famous Big Band musicians, including Jess Stacey, famous pianist with the Benny Goodman trio and band. It was only natural that every summer the excursion boats like the Capitol, would make their annual visits to Cape Girardeau for Moonlight Excursions. These boats would always feature Dixie Land Jazz bands that Grandpa liked.

Grandpa loved to waltz, and on a number of occasions won prizes for the best waltz with a partner by the name of Paula. Paula was just a little shorter than Grandpa and they made a striking couple as they waltzed together. They were never romantically involved. They were just good dancing partners who loved to dance with each other. Grandpa says, "Ballroom dancing was one of the most enjoyable experiences in my youth."

Life was not all fun. Things happened that were beyond the control of either Grandpa, his classmates, or his teachers. Grandpa says, "There is a 'flip' side to every experience, and it was true of my high school days. There were serious and tragic events that happened." A young man dived into a swimming hole and hit his head on a rock. He had brain and neck injury. After several days of anxious watching and waiting by his parents and the entire student body, he died without regaining consciousness. He was an honor student, highly respected, and far too young to die. The student body was shocked and suddenly made aware of how fragile life really is. It seemed to be so meaningless and there were no easy answers. Students wrestled with the question, "Why?"

A girl in the junior class became seriously ill. She spent a long period of time in the hospital and then spent many months in her home seeking to recover. She was a very popular student and was visited often in her home by Grandpa and other students. She deeply regretted that she smoked and stayed out late at night and felt she did not get proper rest, and this was at least partially responsible for her illness. She always urged her friends not to smoke and to get proper rest. It became apparent she was not recovering. One morning when Grandpa arrived at the school, he was informed of her death. Again, the entire student body struggled with the question, "Why?"

One of the most shocking experience came when a very beautiful girl from a prominent family took her own life. The students reacted in unbelief. They felt it just couldn't be possible that such a happy, popular girl could come to such a tragic death so early in life. "Why?"

During the fun years and through these tragic experiences Grandpa struggled with a deep inner voice that reminded him of the call to preach the unsearchable riches of Christ. This nagging call was always in the deep subconscious of Grandpa's being. He knew there were no easy answers to the deep questions of life, but there was a growing conviction that the only place to find understanding was in faith in Jesus Christ. He still pushed the call back into the subconscious. He was not yet ready to be fully obedient to God's claim upon his life.

During his senior year Grandpa fell in love with the E flat alto saxophone and practiced daily. He especially wanted to play arrangements of the big bands. Shortly after graduating from high school at 16 years of age, he organized a 10 piece dance band and began playing professionally all over Southeast Missouri, Southern Illinois and Kentucky. Grandpa and the band became very popular in that area. He dreamed of a big band career. Grandpa and his band broadcast for many weeks from the Rainbow Room of the Idanha Hotel in Cape Girardeau. Members of the band were recruited from old high school friends, the Southeast Missouri State College, and other towns in the area.

The band owned a trailer, a P.A. system, eight decorated music stands with Grandpa's name on the front, and a good repertoire of musical arrangements. The pianist and a trumpet player wrote many of the musical arrangements the band played, as well as some original songs. Grandpa directed the band, played saxophone, and was the vocal soloist for the band. All of the members of the band sang as a male choral group. Most of the engagements were played within a hundred mile radius of Cape Girardeau, in dance halls and nightclubs located in the many small towns throughout the area. The boys would load up the trailer and drive out to these towns in two old cars, with one car pulling the trailer. It was an exciting way of life and they met many interesting people. They usually played until midnight or one a.m. and then loaded up the trailer and headed back home. There was a celebrity status that fans of the band provided that gave musicians an exaggerated sense of self-worth.

It was a real miracle that Grandpa did not wind up with serious problems during these years. There were many temptations that tested the values implanted by his family, his church, and his school. Grandpa used the trial and error method of testing these values. Drugs were no problem in those days. Grandpa never saw, or heard, of any one who used drugs. However, alcohol was another story. During his high school years and the years that followed, while playing in the dance band, it was an ever present social pressure. Admiring fans always were ready to provide a drink. Grandpa experimented a few times. However, the values that were instilled in his early years, along with the fact that he hated the taste of beer, wine and alcohol, gave him the strength to withstand the pressure. Grandpa says, "To drink something you don't like, and that will make a fool out of you, is sheer stupidity." It was rather unusual that not one member of the band drank beer or any other form of alcohol. Tobacco was another constant temptation that was placed before Grandpa by advertising and social pressure from fans. Grandpa tried cigarettes and cigars that were supposed to make you a man of distinction. Grandpa says, "It never made me feel distinguished, it only made me smell like stale tobacco. I hated the taste and the smell of tobacco either first-hand or secondhand." Girls who smelled like stale tobacco soon lost their appeal as far as Grandpa was concerned.

Some of Grandpa's friends liked to gamble. This too, had no appeal for Grandpa who says, "If you gamble, you are either a thief or a fool. If you get something for nothing you are a thief, and if you get nothing for something you are a fool." Grandpa often heard his dad make this statement and it made a lasting impression.

Girls and sex were a different story. Sex is the most difficult drive to discipline. It is the most difficult to understand in a meaningful way. Grandpa discovered very quickly that sexual desire is just as difficult for girls to control as it is for boys. The sexual drive is one of God's most wonderful gifts to persons to be used in the context of marriage, for recreation of life, and to provide an atmosphere of love in the home where children are raised. When we understand its purpose we are better able to understand how to discipline it. There is either discipline or disaster in the lives of teenagers who are not ready to accept the responsibilities of being parents (This is a much greater problem today). Grandpa says, "I made my share of mistakes, and I am grateful that I came through those turbulent years without a major problem. I was a very imperfect youth with many faults and failures. I credit my parents' love and patience, my teachers, and God's grace for saving me from a disaster such as a teen age pregnancy, alcoholism, or tobacco addiction, during those turbulent years. Six things helped me keep a delicate balance in my life and guided me through those difficult years:

Church!

      I kept going to church nearly every Sunday.

      I went to Sunday School and Epworth League.

Family!

      I tried to remember the values of my home.

      I admitted the things I did that were wrong.

Forgiveness!

      I asked God to forgive me.

      I cultivated a sense of humor and

Humor!

      Was able to laugh at myself

Grandpa says, "The primary responsibility to teach children about the God given gift of the sex drive and desire, lies with parents. I certainly do not know all the answers. No one does, because all knowledge is in part. I do have some suggestions for parents after many years of experience and careful thought."

"Teach your children the truth in love (God's love), as you understand the truth. The following facts are important for your children to know.

1. The sexual desire they feel is normal and shared by the whole of humanity.

2. Sexual desire is good. It brings real pleasure and meaning to life (even to you as a parent), when used properly.

3. Sex is a gift of God for the specific purpose of recreating life (babies), and to create an atmosphere of love in the home in which to raise children.

4. Teen age youth are not ready for the responsibility of being parents.

5. Encourage your children to ask questions about parental responsibilities. Are you ready to change diapers, cleanup stool urine? Make car payments? Pay rent? Stay home night after night with the same guy or gal and baby? You can continue to add to the list.

6. Facts about the dangers of sexual disease, AIDS, syphilis, and gonorrhea, etc. Don't try to scare, but be brutally frank. This may seem tough, but not as tough as many of the problems that happen to our youth when they face temptations without proper information.

Five year old Mary was playing daily with six year old Jimmie. One day Jimmie told his mother that he and Mary were going to get married. His mother immediately replied, "You are not old enough to get married, there is a lot of responsibility that goes with marriage." Jimmie says, "We have talked about that and we still want to get married. His mother said, "Jimmie, you have to provide a place to live." "We have figured it out. We are going to live in Mary's playhouse," said Jimmie. His mother replied, "There may be babies." Jimmie said, "We thought about that. We are going to watch real close and every time she lays an egg we are going to step on it." That is a funny story that is to be expected of a five and six years old boy and girl, but it is inexcusable in a teenager. However, many teenager's make important decisions that lack factual information that is as naïve as the decision by the five and six year old. It is the responsibility of parents to teach their boys and girls facts about sex. If you teach your son or daughter the facts as you know them and they fall, don't blame yourself. The responsibility to use those facts in making an intelligent decision is theirs.

Grandpa says, "I am so grateful for my teen years. The rewards of those years were many. I learned how to make decisions on my own. I became more confident about who I am as a person. I learned to think in a logical way about the important truths in my life. These were some of the most rewarding years of my life." Grandpa declares, "The most important and rewarding thing happened when I was 19, the final year of my teens. I met a beautiful, brown eyed girl, with auburn hair, and fell madly in love with her. I met Grandma, and she changed the course of my life forever."

Grandpa says: "Grandma has polished me to
perfection/almost."

CHAPTER 5
GRANDMA

Grandpa is perfect/almost because of the cooperative efforts of God and Grandma. The only one who has worked longer and harder at the project of trying to improve Grandpa than Grandma is God. He has been trying to perfect Grandpa for more than eighty years. Grandma runs a close second, having volunteered to help God on this project more than sixty years ago. Grandpa is perfect/almost as a result of their long-suffering. This is a gigantic undertaking.

Grandma started at the bottom on this project. She started on the ground floor with Grandpa's shoes. At the beginning of their marriage for some unknown reason, Grandma had Grandpa to take off his shoes every time he came into the house (I think she must have gotten the idea from the experience of Moses at the burning bush. God told Moses to pull off his shoes, he was standing on holy ground. Grandma declared the house as holy ground for Grandpa). As soon as Grandpa took his shoes off Grandma would immediately wash the bottoms and clean and polish them to perfection. Grandpa says, "I was known as the preacher with the best shined shoes in the Annual Conference (You see, this is not all bad)." One Sunday Grandpa preached a sermon on love and made a point that love does some things because it wants to, and not because it has to. He used the story about Grandma polishing his shoes and said, "I have never once asked her to shine my shoes. She simply does it because she loves me and wants me to look my best." He then commented "If we really love God, there are many things we will do, simply because we are grateful and love him, not because he requires them." After the service a woman said to Grandpa, "You don't need to think I'm going to shine my husband's shoes just because your wife does." Several other women made similar comments (of course they missed the point). Grandma continued to shine Grandpa's shoes for nearly fifty years because she wanted to do so.

Shortly after the Bishop appointed Grandpa to be a District Superintendent, Grandpa noticed his shoes were not being shined as usual. After a couple of weeks, Grandpa asked Grandma why his shoes were no longer being shined. Very quickly Grandma answered, "Oh, didn't you know, I received a promotion? I am now the wife of a District Superintendent." Grandpa smiled and has been shining his own shoes ever since. A good thing had finally come to an end. Grandpa said, "I have learned over the years that a man is never neatly dressed unless his shoes are shined."

Perhaps you are beginning to understand why Grandpa is perfect/almost. Grandma is an angel on a mission with God striving to perfect Grandpa. She is doing her thing quite effectively. The task is not completed but she just keeps persevering.

Grandma not only started at the bottom with Grandpa's shoes, she also went to the top (the top of Grandpa's head, that is). Grandpa had a lot of dark brown hair when he was young and had a couple of big waves on the right side. However, he also had a cowlick on the left side that gave him a lot of trouble in keeping it combed properly.

Grandma immediately went to work in reminding Grandpa how to remedy the problem. It is a very persistent problem that did not respond too quickly to Grandma's remedies. It resisted Grandma's tender loving care until Grandpa was 70 years old and it was no longer a problem because his hair got so thin and white you couldn't tell there was a cowlick. Grandma felt a deep sense of accomplishment because there was no longer a problem. Grandma, God, and age were polishing Grandpa to perfection/almost.

Grandma's mission was not quite complete, however. Grandpa also had a problem that did not subside with the aging process. Grandpa had hair on the back of his head that was unruly and by nature wanted to stick out (at eighty you are happy to have any kind of hair, anywhere, that will stick out). Grandma has brushed that hair down ten thousand times. Every time Grandpa is ready to leave the house she sends him back to the bathroom to wet it down and brush it down. Grandpa says that, "All the grains of sand on the beach cannot compare to the number of times she has told him to brush down his hair in the back." Grandma will surely have a lot of stars in her crown for trying so hard to polish Grandpa's hair to perfection/almost (The twigs are still sticking out in back). Grandma still inspects it every time Grandpa leaves the house.

Grandpa says, "I have learned, over these many years, that the well-groomed man must not have a hair out of place (I earnestly pray that someday I shall reach perfection because Grandma worked so hard)."

Grandma is aware of when Grandpa needs a haircut and reminds him it is time to call the barber shop for an appointment. Grandpa says, "I have learned, that if I am to look proper and meet Grandma's specifications, I must keep my hair trimmed to the proper length, and the timing is crucial."

Grandma is well-versed in how to instruct the barber as to how Grandpa should have his hair cut, length of the sideburns, etc. It is easy to see why Grandpa is perfect/almost. Grandpa says, "I feel sorry for those guys who are on their own and don't have a best friend to help get all these things done at the right time." Grandma keeps real busy doing her thing, "polishing Grandpa." He fusses about it, but he loves it. Grandpa says, "I know she loves me, otherwise she wouldn't spend so much time and energy on me."

Grandma is not only interested in what Grandpa's head looks like, she is interested in what is on the inside, and what comes out of it. Grandma is Grandpa's best critic of the sermons he preaches (Especially his grammar and the pronunciation of words). Grandpa says, "I have the degrees, Grandma has the knowledge. She is an avid reader and is involved in education as a lifetime process." When Grandpa makes mistakes, Grandma has a way of telling him that he can understand. One time during the Lenten season, Grandpa was eloquently proclaiming the biblical account of the transfiguration of Jesus. Several times he pronounced it "transfigurization." Later Grandma shocked Grandpa when she said, "When you pronounced it wrong the first time it wasn't so bad. Most people probably thought it was a slip of the tongue, but when you did it two more times they knew it was pure stupidity." Grandpa got the picture quickly and began to shape up (He also made a mental note on how Grandma painted a graphic word picture that communicates). Many times Grandpa made the mistake and Grandma did the correcting. Grandpa says, "Anyone can see why I am perfect/almost."

When they lay Grandpa in a casket Grandma will pray the following prayer:

Dear Lord,
This is Grandma, and here is Grandpa.

I have done the best I could with him.

I have worked as hard as I could for over 60 years.

It has been a very difficult job and I did not quite finish with him, as I ran out of time.

Grandpa is perfect/almost, and I have really enjoyed trying to shape him up.

Please forgive him where his faults are not polished off, I am to blame.

I also pray you will forgive me for not quite completing my mission.

I now commit him to your never failing love and mercy.

May he rest in peace for all eternity! AMEN!

Grandpa says, "Grandma is the most wonderful and faithful angel God ever assigned to a mission. I am truly grateful to her for faithfully polishing me to perfection/almost, as we traveled together over this long and incredible journey. Without her, life would have had no meaning. She has made the journey a joy!"

CHAPTER 6
A FUN FAMILY

In the beginning laughter was a part of Grandpa and Grandma's marriage. It was a very sacred moment when they stood before the altar of the Methodist Church in Corning, Arkansas. Both Grandpa and Grandma felt this was a once in a life-time experience because they each came from backgrounds with strong beliefs that what God has joined together, man does not put asunder. Death alone parts such a union. However, they smiled as they thought of the name of the minister who received their vows, The Reverend J. Turpin Wilcoxin. As if the name was not enough, he also had a wooden leg. The Reverend was a lovable man of God with a fine voice and a gentle spirit. He did an excellent job. Through the years Grandpa and Grandma look at their license and smile.

Grandpa and Grandma eloped and were married in the presence of close friends, and their best friend, God. It is an understatement to say they shocked all of their family members. A brother-in-law said, "Don't criticize these kids, they are good kids, they are young, but they know what they are doing. They will be just fine." Grandpa thinks he was right. God proved he was right throughout Grandma and Grandpa's incredible journey. The advice of this brother-in-law was good advice and with the support of their families and the help of God, they have had more than 60 years of joy in raising a fun family.

Grandpa says, "I believed we were going to make it and we have. We didn't have to get married, we just wanted to get married. We had no children, by design, for two years. Through those 60 years we have laughed and cried together. We have experienced the good and the bad of life. We rejoiced in the good and learned from the bad. The rewards and the joy have been found in the journey itself."

Grandpa says, "If I had it to do over again, I would do it exactly the same way. God was present in that union, it was less work and worry than a big church wedding, and it sure was less of a financial burden on our families." A little humor has helped bring balance into Grandpa and Grandma's relationship through the years and has carried them over many miles of their long and incredible journey. Grandpa says, "It is not the size or the cost of a wedding that measures the success of the relationship, but the depth of the commitment of the two people to each other and to God. Marriage must be built on eternal values."

Shortly after their marriage they took a fun trip with Grandma's brother and his wife (Also newlyweds). Grandpa's dad loaned them his new black Pontiac with two yellow spare wheels and tires that sat in the front fenders on both sides (Notice his Dad's support). It was truly a beauty, and Grandpa thought it was the most fantastic car that General Motors ever built. The two couples were going to visit Grandma's relatives in Kentucky. They were going to stay with Grandma's Uncle Simon, who had a large farm house not far from the banks of the Ohio River. As they drove along having a good time, Grandpa made a slip of the tongue and called Grandma's uncle, Uncle Salmon (Canned salmon). Everyone roared with laughter, and for the rest of the trip, Grandpa called him Uncle Salmon. Grandpa and Grandma's brother loved to sing old gospel songs and popular songs as they rolled along. Once in a while Grandpa would say, "I bet Uncle Salmon is sure glad we're coming!" Everyone laughed and they warned Grandpa that if he wasn't careful he would forget and call him Uncle Salmon to his face. However, Grandpa paid no attention to the warning. Guess what? You guessed right. The first morning at the breakfast table Grandpa said, "Uncle Salmon would you please pass the ham." Grandma was really aggravated, and if looks could have killed, Grandpa would have died at an early age and their marriage would have been short-lived. However, he survived, and no one seemed to notice. Everyone really enjoyed the ham, biscuits, gravy, and all the other good things Uncle Simon's wife had so graciously prepared. It was a real fun family get together.

Grandma wanted to visit her old home town in Sturgis, Kentucky. They inquired as to the best way to go, and were told there were two ways to go. One was up the river road that was very rough, or another route that was a much better road but was 25 miles further. After talking it over they decided to take the shorter route. Wow! Was it ever rough. Every hundred feet or so, you would jump off a bench rock, and it was unbelievable how rough it was. Before reaching the highway they had two flat tires, and much to Grandpa's consternation both of the two yellow wheels and spare tires had to be removed from the front fenders to replace the flat tires. It was a hot day, causing Grandpa to sweat and worry about what Dad would say when they got home with two tires ruined on his new car. They all had to laugh to keep from crying. Finally, they covered the 25 miles of rough road and made the rest of the journey safely. Needless to say, they took the longer route back. In spite of the flat tires, they all had a ball. Grandma showed Grandpa where she lived as a small girl in Sturgis, where she went to church, where she played, and many other places that had special meaning for her. All along the route they traveled, she pointed out where her many relatives lived (an unbelievable number).

When they got back from the long but enjoyable trip, Uncle Simon (Salmon) was still there, gracious host that he was, waiting to make their visit a time they would never forget. Uncle Simon and his wife made the trip a fun experience. He took them for a ride in a farm wagon, pulled by a beautiful team of horses. The trip covered the entire farm. They saw the hogs and pigs, the cattle and the beautiful white chickens they raised. He took them up to the top of the bluff end showed them the pasture land and the many head of cattle that grazed there (The bluff overlooked the beautiful Ohio River). He proudly displayed the river bottom land where they raised their crops. It was an ideal family farm, and they were a wonderful family to care for it and to reap its rich harvest. It was quite apparent Uncle Simon loved the farm and was indeed proud of his farm and the tradition of family farms to which he belonged. Grandma's brother farmed with Uncle Simon, and Grandpa had a wonderful time getting acquainted with him, his wife, and their son. Good families are a great blessing and wonder to enjoy and to share.

When they headed for home, it was with a feeling of regret that they had to leave after enjoying a week with some of Grandma's good family. Grandpa says, "Grandma and I are proud of the two typical American families from whence we came. We are truly proud of our families and the fun they provide, a fun family."

Grandpa and Grandma really had fun in their first two room apartment. It was on the second floor of a nice home on a large lot next to the Southeast Missouri State University (It is now a part of the campus). The home was owned by a long time friend of Grandpa's family. The apartment had a combined living and bedroom, and a large kitchen and dining area. It was furnished, including a two burner oil cook stove with a small portable oven. Grandma had not had much experience in cooking, as Grandpa soon found out. The cooking stove didn't give her much incentive or help, but she learned to be a good cook in a hurry with a few major problems along the way.

One pay day Grandpa stopped to get a haircut after getting off work (He was working at a shoe factory). This made him late for dinner. When he arrived home, Grandma was sitting at the kitchen table crying. When he inquired as to the problem, her anger with him was quite apparent (Some angels do have a temper). She was really sobbing as she said, "I made you some biscuits, and they were not too bad when they first came out of the oven (Questionable). I have waited so long, and they are so hard you can't eat them." Well, Grandpa sat down and ate them all. He almost broke several of his teeth, and he had indigestion for two days and nights. Grandpa says, "it's the gospel truth, if I would have dropped one of them, they were so hard they would have made a hole in the floor." Grandpa never let Grandma know that he had indigestion or how hard they were. They have had many a laugh over Grandma's first biscuits made in a portable oven on a two burner stove in their first apartment. Grandpa says, "Laughter is an absolute necessity as a balance of life. It saves a lot of marriages, including ours.

In those days there was no air conditioning, and it gets awfully hot on the second floor in a two room apartment when the temperature gets above 90 degrees. Grandpa says, "That is especially true when you have two young people madly in love and passions are running high." Well, Grandpa and Grandma did the sensible thing and took a couple of blankets and slept outdoors on the back lawn of this fine home next to the University in the month of July. It provided comfort and a wonderful place for Grandma and Grandpa to make love.

Grandpa says, "That first year in a two room furnished apartment was one of the happiest and fun times of our long and fruitful marriage."

During that first year Grandpa and Grandma started saving money to purchase furniture. Grandma served as the bank and personally kept the savings safe (Hopefully). One day Grandpa came home from work and Grandma was in distress and crying. Grandma and a friend, who had a baby, went for a walk downtown pushing the baby in a buggy. Grandma lost her pocketbook. It had everything they owned in it, including their savings of one hundred and twenty-five dollars. Her name was not in the pocketbook. She was sure it would never be returned. Grandpa said, "Just calm down, there are a lot of honest people in the world. Some way or another we will get it back." Grandpa thought of an old friend who was a local news announcer on radio station K.F.V.S. Grandpa called and told the announcer about the incident. He announced it on the six o'clock news. He had hardly finished when the telephone rang. It was a barber on Broadway who had seen Grandma drop her purse. By the time he got out of the shop and picked up the purse, Grandma was gone. The money was returned in full. It was a time of rejoicing, and Grandma's faith in mankind was restored. At that time, at least she was glad she had Grandpa and was thankful for his friend, the K.F.V.S. news reporter. God's goodness works through ordinary people like the barber and the reporter. Later Grandpa and Grandma purchased a new bedroom suite that they kept throughout most of their married life. All their children were conceived on that bed. They later gave it to their youngest son, and his two children were conceived on the same bed. It was quite a bed with productive and lasting qualities.

Grandpa's fist car, a 1930 V8 Ford was a lemon. He didn't know a thing about buying a car. He "kicked the tires," and it seemed to pass the test. It didn't fall apart so he was convinced it was a good car, and besides, it was cheap. After six or eight weeks with nothing but expenses (Major problems), the car salesman would do nothing about it. He said, "You bought it 'as is,' it's yours." Grandpa finally took it back and left it on the lot as a gift to the salesman. He chalked it up as a learning experience and decided that a car had to pass some kind of test other than "kicking the tires."

Grandpa's second car was a Model A Sports Roadster with a rumble seat. It was a real beauty and was Grandpa and Grandma's pride and joy. It was really sporty and they were the envy of all the young couples they knew. Before Grandpa purchased it, he took it to a mechanic friend who drove it and checked it out. His friend said, "As far as I can tell it is in good shape and it doesn't have too many miles on it (Grandpa was learning)." The Model A proved to be as good as their first car was bad. That Model A brought many fun experiences to Grandma and Grandpa. They would put their two little guys in the rumble seat and away they would go. One day Grandma was taking Grandpa to work. They were traveling east on Broadway, which was a very narrow street in spite of its broad name. They approached a beer truck stopped in their lane to unload at a restaurant. Another large, beautiful new Chrysler was traveling west in the other lane. Grandma started to pull up behind the truck and stop. Grandpa said, "Don't stop here, there is plenty of room to go around." Grandma did what he suggested and scraped the Chrysler all down the side. Grandpa fumed and fussed, and Grandma cried. It was Grandpa's fault. They had to pay for having the side of the

Chrysler refinished. That took some of the fun out of the Model A, and Grandma never again obeyed Grandpa when she was driving (Even though she had promised to "love and obey").

One of their favorite trips in the Model A was to Grandma's sister who lived in Kentucky. Her husband was a fun guy who loved Grandpa and Grandma's kids. He loved to play with them even though they were very small. The kids were crazy about him. The boys, who were three and four years old, loved the open fireplaces with which they heated the house. They loved the out house, the cows, the chickens, and the horses their uncle would let them ride as he led them.

One time Grandpa and Grandma loaded them up in the Model A to go to their uncle and aunt's house in Kentucky for a week's vacation. Grandpa and his dad were building a house, and it was necessary for him to return home. During that week, the Ohio River went out of its bank to a record breaking flood stage. When Grandpa returned for them on Sunday, the roads into the farm were closed and he couldn't get to the farm house in the Model A. In a telephone conversation, Uncle told Grandpa to wait and he would bring them out in a high wheeled wagon and meet him on the main road. Uncle hitched up a wagon with high wheels and drove through the higher fields where the water was two or three feet deep. With the high wheeled wagon, he was able to bring them out to where Grandpa was waiting with the Model A. They transferred Grandma and the boys, along with their clothes, into the Model A, and they were soon on their way home. That was a fun filled adventure the boys would never forget (Neither would Grandpa and Grandma).

The kids were always a source of fun and enjoyment in Grandpa and Grandma's family. When the two older boys were about two and three years of age, the family was living in the second house Grandpa had built for them on old Highway 61, known as the Highway of Roses. One day Grandma was bathing the boys and had finished with the three year old and was finishing up with the younger one. She looked up and the older one had gotten out of the house and was running across the yard to his Grandmother's house as nude as a jay bird. All the people driving along the Highway of Roses could see the rosy cheeks of the bare butt of a three year old nude boy. Grandma took out after him and when she caught him, she wrapped him in a towel and headed back to the house deeply embarrassed, but also laughing. There was never a dull moment in Grandma and Grandpa's family. It is a wonderful experience to belong to a good, fun family.

One Sunday morning, Grandpa and his oldest son were breezing along toward Owenton, Kentucky. All at once a car wheel passed them on the shoulder of the highway. Grandpa's son said, "Dad l think our wheel just passed us." He was right, of course, and Grandpa felt the car settle down a little on the right rear side. He managed to get safely off the road and got out of the car to look things over. They walked up the road and retrieved the wheel. Grandpa managed to get the back end of the car jacked up. Everything seemed to be okay. The only problem was the lug bolts had come loose and were nowhere to be found. Grandpa was due to preach in about 30 minutes at the Owenton Church. Grandpa said, "I don't think we are going to make it. I'm going to be late." About that time his five year old son said, "Dad, why don't you take one lug bolt off of each of the other wheels and use them." He was an angel on a mission from God to help Grandpa when he needed it. Grandpa was embarrassed to take advice from a five year old boy, but he did. It worked, and they were soon in Owenton at the church with 10 minutes to spare. Grandpa had many a good laugh over that incident and so has the rest of the family. Grandpa says, "I never thought of my oldest son as an angel very often but I did that day." Sometimes people fail to recognize that their own children often speak words of wisdom.

During Grandpa's appointment to Divernon, Glenarm and Farmersville Churches, the family took a real vacation for the first time (The family was unable to afford one before that time). Ever since then, vacations have been a real source of fun for Grandpa and Grandma's family. That first two weeks was spent at the Lake of the Ozark Resort. During that vacation, Grandpa and Grandma and their kids met a wonderful family from a small town in Iowa, where the father published a newspaper. The families enjoyed each other's company and by intentional planning, they started coming to the same resort at the same time each year. They were a fun family, and both families enjoyed many of the same things. The two families went to the same resort for a number of years.

While on vacation, Grandpa and Grandma never told the new people they met that Grandpa was a preacher. They wanted to get to know the new people without them putting on a facade that people often do in the presence of a preacher. This provided many fun experiences when people would find out later. This was true of the family from Iowa. Their children were nearly the same age as Grandpa and Grandma's kids, and a real bond of friendship developed. They loved to swim, fish, and water ski together. Many meals were shared as well as an occasional picnic, shopping or sightseeing trip. Sometimes in the evenings, they would attend one of the many entertainment attractions, such as the Ozark Opera, a country music show that they all enjoyed. It was great fun to share together.

The third summer they were enjoying a picnic, when the father looked at Grandpa and asked a direct question, "What is your profession? You never have told us." Grandpa could no longer avoid the issue. He said, "I am a clergyman." The other family were Methodists. The father immediately started to apologize for all the things they had said or done that they felt they should not have done in the presence of a clergyman and his family. Grandpa assured him that they had been doing just fine and urged them to relax and keep being themselves just as they had done for the past two years. He told him no apology was necessary for anything. The friendship continued to grow, and they often laughed about the experience.

Harry and May, the owners of the resort, did not know for several years that Grandpa was a preacher. One year Grandpa and Grandma took a bus load of about 35 kids from Divernon United Methodist Church on a one week's trip to the Lake of the Ozarks. Half of them stayed at Harry and May's Lake of the Ozark Resort, and the other half at a resort across the road. When they unloaded, Harry heard one of the kids call Grandpa, Reverend. Embarrassed, he rushed into the resort and said to May, "My God, May, he is a Methodist preacher. What in the hell have I done in front of him and his kids that I shouldn't have?" Grandpa and Grandma's kids worshiped Harry and May, and Harry and May loved the kids ardently. They had no children of their own. Harry was quite a beer drinker and always had a bottle of beer in his hand during hot weather. He later apologized to Grandpa and Grandma. Grandma assured him that everything was fine and not to worry and to just relax! He said, "If you would have told me, I would have been different." Grandpa said, "Harry, I intentionally did-n't tell you because we would never have really gotten to know you and May if I had told you. We would not have become such good friends. Just relax and be yourself." The friendship continued for many years. Several years after this incident occurred, Harry and May visited Grandpa and Grandma in Illinois and sent a gift to their daughter at the time of her wedding. May became a good member of the Lake of the Ozark Church and sang in the choir, largely through Grandpa and Grandma's influence. Harry was baptized and joined the church before his death. Both have been dead for many years. Grandpa and Grandma counted them both as very good friends. The kids will always remember those summers of family fun. Grandpa says, "Those were fun years with many rewards. I learned that some of my most fruitful ministry was accomplished while my family and I were having fun outside the walls of the sanctuary. Some of my least effective work was among some of the saints. Fun is a necessity to keep a delicate balance in the life of a minister and his family."

One time the family was leaving the Ozark Resort area after a two week vacation and were filling the car with gas for the return trip home. Grandpa and his daughter were waiting in line to pay the bill at the cash register. While waiting, they were looking over some of the humorous postcards in a display rack. Both of them really got tickled at one of the cards and were laughing quite boisterously as they left the station. When they reached the car, Grandma immediately reprimanded them for being so loud and wanted to know what was so funny. Grandpa explained that a card on the rack had a woman and about five kids lined up in front of a fenced area watching a zebra. The smallest child was holding his mother's hand, and the others were lined up holding hands according to height in stair-step order. They appeared to be from two to seven years of age. Off to one side, an older brother stood in front of a birdcage. A sign overhead said, "Stork." Inside a circle were the following words expressing the boy's thoughts, "I bet mom is sure glad they have you in here." As we drove away all of the family was laughing with the exception of the youngest son. When things quieted down he softly said, "Mom, I don't see anything funny about that." Everyone burst into laughter. Grandma eloquently explained things to him. They drove on with everyone quiet. No one spoke. After about fifteen minutes, the small fry spoke up again., "Mom, I still don't see anything funny about that." Everyone burst into laughter again. Grandma tried again, and in a very detailed way explained about the birds and the bees and all that good stuff. Grandpa thought, "Boy, she is doing a great job," and he was glad Grandma was doing the explaining instead of him. After about 30 minutes, when everyone had seemingly forgotten the matter, for the third time, a small voice said, "Mom, I still don't see anything funny about that." Grandma never said a word. No one else spoke or laughed. Enough is enough! Grandpa says, "Parents have a difficult role to fill and even the wisest find themselves at times without adequate words. Sometimes silence is the best teacher."

"Land A Livin" was the name Grandpa and Grandma chose for their vacation home on Kentucky Lake where their family spent many happy hours. There is an interesting story of how it came into being. Grandpa was serving as a pastor of "Ole First Church" in Rock Island, Illinois, when he and Grandma took a trip through the Smoky Mountains. On the way home, they planned to meet some good friends from East Peoria First Church, where he formerly served as pastor. They were to meet at Kentucky Lake State Park, near Murray, Kentucky. As they entered the State of Kentucky, Grandpa noticed a number of signs advertising Kentucky Lake lots for sale. Grandpa grew curious and when they approached the road that led to the development area, there was a huge sign designating the way to the Development Office. It looked irresistible, so Grandpa turned off to take a look. Grandma said, "Why did we turn, and where are we going?" Grandpa said, "On a little adventure." There was more truth than poetry in his statement. When they drove up to the office, a salesman met them and offered to take them on a tour of the area and they accepted. They fell in love with the area, which was located near Murray, Kentucky. It was wooded hills over-looking Kentucky Lake. Grandpa and Grandma purchased seven lots all located together near a fresh water spring before leaving.

Grandpa and Grandma were about four hours late in joining their friends at Kentucky Lake State Park. As they enjoyed fresh fish cooked over an open fire, they explained their being late and their exciting adventure and invest-ment. One of their friends, a retired research engineer for the Caterpillar Tractor Company, wanted to visit the development site. The next morning the engineer and his wife left the camp with Grandma and Grandpa and spent most of the day looking over the development. He and his wife also fell in love with the area. Both families purchased a large plot of ground across the road from each other that their families developed as vacation homes. Grandpa sold the original lots he had purchased and made a profit on them that paid for the new plot. This was the beginning of a fun adventure for Grandpa and Grandma that brought many happy vacations for their family and continued to draw the family closer together.

The research engineer had a handicap. He was struck by polio when he was a young man and walked with a crutch. Grandpa says, "This man was one of the closest friends I ever had and I learned so much about under-standing people with a handicap. It was one of the greatest learning experiences of my life. Sometimes when we worked or fished together I almost wished I had a crutch." He had overcome his handicap by learning to use it. Grandma and the research engineer's wife were also very compatible and enjoyed a wonderful relationship. A rewarding friendship developed between their families. The children and grandchildren enjoyed many happy hours together at "Land A Livin."

Grandpa and Grandma and their children built their vacation home. One of the sons-in-law worked very hard in helping Grandpa clear the woods where the house was built. The woods was filled with poison oak. Grandpa was very careful about handling it as they cleared the site. The son-in-law, who was a farmer, boasted, "I work around poison oak and poison ivy all the time and I never get infected." The next week his eyes were swollen shut, and the rash just about covered his body. He had to be taken to the Emergency Room of the hospital for treatment. It became a standing joke with the family, and the son-in-law never lived it down.

One day Grandpa and Grandma and their neighbors were hauling gravel for their driveways. The engineer was looking on and telling the other three how to shovel the gravel (He was always an exceptional boss who knew how to engineer every project). A man came by on a motorcycle and saw the women shoveling gravel. He turned around, came back and stopped. He jumped off his bike, grabbed Grandma's shovel and said, "Lady, you shouldn't be shoveling gravel in this hot weather." He never said a word to the engineer's wife who was also shoveling gravel. He continued to shovel until the trailer was full. Without saying a word, he jumped on his bike and rode away as quickly as he came (It was a replay of the Bronson television character that was very popular at that time). None of them could understand why he grabbed Grandma's shovel and never said a word to the friend's wife. (Could it have been because Grandma was very trim with a good figure that showed even in her old work clothes, and the friend was plump?). This was a source of good humor and many laughs for a long time to come.

Grandpa bought an outboard motor boat in order that the family could ski. He loved to water ski and so did the rest of the family. Grandpa had the privilege of pulling and teaching his grandkids to ski. Grandpa says, "Water is a great force for good. That is why God made so much of it. One of the greatest thrills of my life came when one of my small grandchildren would come up and sail across the top of the water for the first time."

Like everything else, water has a flip side and a few mishaps occurred. One day Grandpa's friend was pulling him behind his boat, and Grandpa was showing off in front of the grandkids, the rest of the family, and friends. He would ski on one ski, and do other tricks he had learned. His friend was driving the boat as fast as it would go, and he was trying to throw Grandpa off the skis and embarrass him. "Wow' Was this ever fun." They made a wide sweeping turn, and Grandpa was planning to drop off near the family. Instead he ran up on the bank and managed to stay on his feet on the sand until he hit a log laying across the beach. The log threw him head first into the sand, and he turned end-for-end several times before coming to a sudden stop. His family and friends, including his friend driving the boat, thought Grandpa was dead. The neighbor cried and said, "I killed him." However, Grandpa was able to get up. He was skin-burned by the sand and had a dislocated right shoulder that caused him to cry out from excruciating pain. As fast as possible, they got him to the boat dock and headed for the Murray Hospital.

Grandpa was really in pain. In order not to cry and complain, he told funny stories (Clean funny stories were always important in Grandpa's life). All of the family thought it was not the time for him to be telling stories. Grandpa told a story about his neighbor. "My friend bought a new mattress. We were hauling the old one to the Salvation Army in Murray on his old trailer. We looked back and the wind was whipping the mattress up and down. My friend said, 'I always did want to make a mattress do that.'" By the time they got to the hospital, they were all ready to murder Grandpa. However, matters got worse. When they got him in the emergency room and gave him a shot for pain, Grandpa told many more stories to the nurses and the doctor while the shoulder was being manipulated back into place. At one point, Grandpa's oldest son got so embarrassed he got up and walked out. The doctor knew Grandpa was a Methodist preacher and asked him what kind of Methodist Grandma was, a praying Methodist or a cussing Methodist? Grandpa immediately replied, "Grandma is a cussing and drinking Methodist." Grandma, who does neither, was thoroughly disgusted with Grandpa, but she hung in there with Grandpa as she has always done. The doctor became a good friend and always cared for the family when they needed him while they were at the Land of Livin.

Grandpa's oldest grandson was an ardent fisherman even at the age of eight or nine years of age. He was a natural for Land A Livin and loved it with a passion. He and Grandpa became close friends as they fished and played together. One of the things about this grandson was that he loved to clean fish and was expert at doing it. This really thrilled Grandpa and his neighbor friend. They would come in tired late in the evening after catching a large string of fish, and the grandson would beg to clean them. There was a cleaning table on the dock with plenty of fresh water. He loved to watch the other fishermen come in with their tall tales and catches. Many of the fish were blue gill, and it would take him a couple of hours to clean and fillet them. He loved every minute of it and would really glow when the family bragged on him and told everyone how skillful he was at cleaning and filleting fish (He now lives in Mississippi and is a commercial pilot). Recently he and his family were home for the yearly Christmas celebration and he said, "Grandpa, I still love to clean fish. The kids and neighbors still bring their fish to me, and I clean and fillet them." Grandpa says, "The fun we had together as a family at Land A Livin still motivates and blesses our lives. Land A Livin was a great teacher of family values and continues to bind us together as a supportive family. Families that play together stay together." Grandpa continues, "I could write an entire book on the fun experiences we had at Land A Livin and not exhaust the source. I am indeed grateful for those happy days together. They still keep me ticking."

Prince was a large white Collie pup that was given to Grandpa by one of his parishioners from Joseph Chapel Church near Harrodsburg, Kentucky. Prince was the ideal pet for Grandpa's small children. He was a well-built animal with a beautiful coat of long white hair and a very gentle spirit. He never lost patience with the kids regardless of how they treated him. His love for the children was unconditional. Prince earned the right to his name in every sense of the term. He watched over the whole family, and no one ever approached the parsonage without him being aware and informing the rest of the family. He loved to play with the kids. They would throw a stick or a ball and he would immediately retrieve it. When they would toss a ball in the air, he would catch it before it hit the ground. Whenever the kids were around, Prince was there by their side.

Prince had one fault, an insatiable desire to chase cars. Any time a car would pull out of the parsonage drive, Prince would chase it down the highway. Somehow the tires and wheels fascinated him, and he would bark and bite at the turning wheels. Grandpa tried all kinds of things to break him, but nothing worked. One day the inevitable happened, and Prince was killed by one of the cars he chased. It was a sad day for the family. Grandpa thought for a while he was going to have to bury the kids and Grandma along with Prince. After burying the dog, the grief continued for days. Every member of the family missed the love and attention that Prince showered on them. Grandpa says, "All the members of our family were a little kinder and had a deeper understanding of the grief through which others passed at the time of death. Prince made a contribution that will never fade."

One of Grandpa's parishioners in the Farmersville Church gave his kids a gift that brought real fun into the lives of every member of the family.

Mary had a little lamb
a pet t'was born to be.
To Grandpa's kids she gave it
and filled them all with glee.

The lamb was named Jimmie
and it fit him to a "T."
He cleanly mowed the lawn,
quite a sight he was to see.

The lamb loved the kids
as anyone could see.
One little fault had Jimmie,'
he butted behind the knees.

Each day the lamb grew bigger
until he became a sheep.
He butted the kids to the ground
and sometimes made them weep.

Grandpa saw t'was time to act,
Mary, he went to see.
They put their heads together,
to market the lamb's fate would be.

Mary in a truck, picked up Jimmie
the kids were sad as could be.
To the market went ole Jimmie
and mutton he soon would be.

To the kids came a check,
they danced and shouted with glee!
The story of the lamb was ended
and life continues, you see!

Grandpa says there's a lesson
as plain as day to see.
Are you aware dear parents,
a sheep your lamb will be?

Grandpa says, "Jimmie added a dimension of growth to
our family and helped us understand that sometimes you
just have to do what you have to do. Mary's gift brought
joy to the life of our family."

Grandpa loved to surprise members of the family with
unexpected and unique gifts. Early in Grandpa and
Grandma's married life, he wanted to surprise Grandma
with a gift. He didn't have much money but he had a deep
desire to get her something special. He began to look everywhere he went. One day while in a store he heard the most

beautiful sound. Upon investigating he found it was coming from a section of the store where they sold pets. He discovered it was coming from a beautiful yellow canary with a small black streak of feathers in each wing. Grandpa stood there struck with awe and said, "Perfect, it is just what I want for Grandma." The bird warbled continuously. Before he left the store, he made a purchase of the bird and a small cage, even though it cost more than he wanted to spend. Grandpa said, "What the heck, it's for Grandma." He got in the old Model A roadster and headed for home with a light heart. Grandpa's feathers fell when he gave it to Grandma. She said, "I don't want an old bird to take care of, it will be messy. I have enough to do without that." She kept the canary and named him "Tim". Tim warbled his way right into her heart. Tim was a real joy! Grandma talked to Tim like he was one of the family. (He actually was). Grandpa often thought she talked to Tim more than she did to him. The two little boys loved Tim and watched him for hours. They especially liked to watch him take a bath. Sometimes when Grandma cleaned Tim's cage, she would release him for a few minutes. This fascinated the boys, and they would try to catch him.

When the family moved into a small furnished apartment when first locating in Louisville, Kentucky, Tim had to be left behind in the care of Grandpa's sister. Several weeks later they received a letter informing them of a tale of tragedy. Little Sister stated that she was really sorry, but while she was cleaning Tim's cage the cat slipped up, caught and devoured him. Grandma and Grandpa both cried. Grandpa said, "Life is full of losses, and as a family we were learning how to handle the disappointments."

Grandpa says, "A fun family is a great blessing. All that I am or ever will become is primarily due to my wife, my kids, my grandchildren, and great-grandchildren. I have learned much from and with them. I am still learning from them at 80 years of age. What fun we have shared together! I am deeply grateful. My family still keeps me ticking."

Grandpa says: "What families celebrate determines the quality of their relationships to one another."

CHAPTER 7
FAMILY CELEBRATIONS

Twenty-six members of Grandpa and Grandma's family and two special friends from the Board of Pensions gathered at a well-known restaurant in Macomb, Illinois, for a gala celebration on March 22, 1996. It was Grandpa and Grandma's 60th wedding anniversary. The celebration was opened by giving thanks to God for his goodness, mercy and love that endures to all generations and led Grandpa and Grandma over the long journey of the past 60 years. The celebrants consumed prime rib beef, with all the trimmings, topped off with a beautiful cake that graced the table. Grandpa and Grandma each spoke a few words. Both were aware that it was only through God's grace and mercy that they survived both the good and the bad on their long journey of faith. Their oldest son spoke a few words of congratulations on behalf of all the members of the family and wished them more happy anniversaries. Their good friend and peer from the Board of Pensions expressed words of congratulations on behalf of the church to which they have given their lives. There was music, laughter, and real joy as children, grandchildren, and great-grandchildren all recognized and honored their grandparents who were responsible for their being brought in to the world. Grandpa kissed Grandma (With all the passion he could muster at 80). He bent her over backward so far they almost fell to the floor.

Grandpa says, "There is nothing I enjoy more than a celebration with my family and friends gathered to share a special occasion. Family celebrations are one of the highest privileges God has given to us. Family celebrations keep me ticking."

Grandpa and Grandma's celebration is a yearly event, not a rare occasion. It is a tradition that Grandpa and Grandma have celebrated every year in some manner or other for the past 60 years. Grandpa feels it is very important to do so. He holds a deep conviction that no marriage will long survive without joyful celebrations of its sacred union.

Grandpa says, "I love family celebrations. Families are created to celebrate events that are common to all members of the family, recognizing their solidarity and support for one another."

Grandpa and Grandma's 56th anniversary was fast approaching. Grandma felt they should not have any kind of formal celebration. She said, "Most people only celebrate their 25th or 50th anniversaries. I think we overdo it by celebrating every year." Grandpa made a mental note of Grandma's comments and formulated a plan. That year the anniversary came on a Sunday. Nothing more was said, and the date rolled around with no preparation being made for a celebration (At least not as far as Grandma knew). Grandpa and Grandma attended worship at First Church, Rushville, Illinois, as was their custom.

A surprise awaited Grandma when they returned home. Grandma noticed several cars in front of their home. They entered the house, and Grandma could not believe her eyes. In the dinning room, the table was tastefully decorated with all the places set, and in the center was a beautiful floral bouquet, ready for a banquet. In the family room a number of couples were waiting to greet and congratulate Grandpa and Grandma. What a joyful surprise! Grandpa had made arrangements with the Bottenburg Inn to cater and serve the dinner, using Grandma's best dishes and silverware, without her knowledge. Grandpa had given them a key, and they were not to come until he and Grandma were gone to Sunday School and worship. Grandma was elated, and Grandpa was as proud as a peacock. It is not easy to surprise Grandma, but this was one of the few times he was really able to surprise her. This was a wonderful day of celebration that will always be remembered. Everyone had a jolly good time including Grandpa and Grandma. Grandpa says, "I never want the surprise element to die in our marriage. It is the spice of life. I can hardly wait until our 61st anniversary to see what new surprise it will bring."

Grandma says, "I never know what to expect. I never know what Grandpa is going to do. Sometimes I have thought about killing him, but for some reason I never have."

Grandpa says, "I think the only reason Grandma hasn't killed me is because she loves the surprise and celebrations."

On May 4, 1986, more than 600 people passed through the reception line at First United Methodist Church to honor Grandpa and Grandma on their 50th wedding anniversary. Their children were the host and hostesses for the occasion. The celebration was late because Grandpa had suffered his first acute heart failure a few months earlier and hovered near death for several weeks. This was the first major illness Grandpa had experienced. Grandpa says, "I rarely took medication and didn't even take aspirins until I was 65 years of age. I had never missed the pulpit on a Sunday because of health until I was 65 years of age." This was a new experience for Grandpa, having neither the strength nor energy to cope with simplest daily task. His doctor, a close friend, did not want Grandpa and Grandma to even try to celebrate their 50th anniversary at all that year. However, Grandpa insisted, and agreed to sit on a kitchen stool in the reception line to greet their friends and former parishioners. Some had come from as far away as Kentucky and Missouri. Grandpa's doctor was present during the entire reception, expecting Grandpa to keel over at anytime. He was a true friend. It was a glorious day, and renewing friendship with so many parishioners and friends was the best medicine Grandpa could have received. Grandpa was very tired and weary when the reception was over, but he loved every minute of it and "hung-in-there" and made it. Grandpa's kids were gracious as they shared memories of the past. A short, humorous history of Grandpa and Grandma's life together was read by their oldest son. What a glorious family celebration it turned out to be. The wedding cake was magnificent, and the United Methodist Women did a superb job in service. Grandpa and Grandma's granddaughters were at the serving table. There were family members from Missouri and Kentucky. What a glorious day of celebration!

Grandpa and Grandma had a wonderful celebration of their 40th anniversary in the Rushville Church. Anniversary celebrations have played an important role in Grandpa and Grandma's marriage. It is a yearly tradition that has helped to shape Grandpa's life and the life of his family.

The central celebration of Grandpa and Grandma's family is worship. Under no circumstances can you understand What Makes Grandpa Tick without seeing the importance of worship and the church. Worship means paying respect and reverence to a divine being. For many years, Grandpa and Grandma have made their way to the church when the sun is shining, when it is raining and snowing, when it is freezing underfoot or whatever conditions exist. They have done this not because they have to do it to get to heaven, or gain divine favor, but because they want to celebrate God's worthiness. Grandpa and Grandma wholeheartedly endorse the words of the writer of the Psalms, "I was glad when they said unto me let us go into the house of the Lord." What a joy to worship when it is not a duty, but a high privilege to give respect and reverence to a God of love, of mercy and goodness that endures to all generations. What a blessing to rejoice in the presence of a good God who loves us in spite of our badness."

In worship we celebrate God's forgiveness which we all need. Grandpa says, "Sometimes as I worship I am reminded that a few days ago I spoke sharp words to Grandma and hurt her feelings. I praise God because He made possible forgiveness through the gift of his son, Jesus, who shed his blood and suffered death on the cross for my sins. Jesus opened the door to God's loving forgiveness and did something for me that I could not do for myself. I make no attempt to give answers to why this is true. I simply believe it and say with the psalmist, 'Have mercy upon me, O God, according to thy loving kindness, according unto thy tender mercies blot our my transgressions.' I think that is something to celebrate." Grandpa and Grandma celebrate God's forgiveness through Christ in worship every Sunday morning in prayer, praise, and fellowship with other Christians.

In worship we celebrate God's cleansing power and indwelling presence. Grandpa says, "In my daily life I discover that my real problem is much deeper than my outward sins. I find something deep inside that causes me, unwillingly, to do things I do not normally want to do. I grow angry, speak a word that hurts, or do something I know is wrong. I have a sinful spirit deep within my being." The psalmist recognizes this and declares, "Behold, thou desires" truth in the inward parts; and in the hidden part thou shalt make me to know wisdom." What a great

112

joy it is to discover God's cleansing power at work deep inside your being, to indwell and make clean your heart. What a privilege it is to celebrate and thank God for His cleansing and indwelling presence that lives and moves in the life of His people. What a joy when we can cry out with the psalmist, "Create in me a clean heart, O God; renew a right spirit within me. Cast me not away from thy presence; and take not thy holy spirit from me." Grandpa and Grandma love to celebrate God's living presence at work in their lives amidst all their imperfections. Grandpa says, "This is celebration at its best. This is really living."

A family church celebration that Grandpa loves most is that of a family wedding. Grandpa has married all of his children but one. When his daughter got married she said, "For once I just want you to be my father and give me away, I also want you to sit with mom." Grandpa felt honored by this request, and though he hated to break a tradition, that is exactly what he did. It was a gala Christmas wedding in First United Methodist Church in Rushville. The church was decorated with poinsettias. The bride's gown was white, and her maid of honor and matrons wore red gowns. Grandpa says, "When I brought my daughter down the aisle it was a high moment in which I felt pride, a warm and fuzzy feeling, and I experienced the high privilege of being her father in a new way. What a joyous celebration." Son One and Son Two were married in church weddings in the Rushville Church. Grandpa married Son Four in First United Methodist Church in Victor, Iowa, the church of the bride. All of these weddings were wonderful times of celebration that strengthened the family as a close knit group. Families are supportive of one another when they celebrate together in the church. Grandpa has united seven grandchildren in church weddings (Two more to go). These were all joyous occasions. Grandpa has also baptized six of his great-grandchildren with joy and excitement shared by family members. Grandpa says, "When you hold the soft and warm, small body of one of your own flesh and blood, and baptize that child in the name of the Father, Son, and Holy Spirit, it is one of life's most fulfilling experiences."

Tomorrow morning Grandpa and Grandma will make their way to the church. It will be the first Sunday of the month, and they will join several hundred other persons in celebrating Holy Communion. The pastor will break a loaf of bread and repeat the words Jesus spoke that last night to his disciples as they celebrated his approaching death, "This is my body that is broken for you." The pastor will lift the cup and again repeat the words of Jesus, "This is my blood of the New Covenant that was shed for you." Grandpa and Grandma will join with the people and partake of the elements remembering the supreme sacrifice that Christ made that they might know God's love, forgiveness, and His living presence that brings hope and a quality of life that is eternal. Grandpa will remember the many times that his wife and four children knelt at the altar of the churches he served and received the elements of Holy Communion from his hands. Grandpa says, "I always remember my own unworthiness, and am grateful for God's supreme sacrifice. I know this is a very solemn and sorrowful occasion as I remember the suffering of our Lord, and my sins that caused the suffering. However, I know it is a very joyful celebration of hope as I receive forgiveness for my sins made possible through the cross." This is a joyful celebration because it binds families together by indelibly planting memories in the subconscious mind that cannot be erased."

Family celebrations bring a lively hope of a quality of life called eternal. Christ's death and sufferings were not the final chapter. There is an open tomb with victory over the experience of death. Grandpa says, "This brings the hope of the victory of life over death to all of us. It is the gift of God. That is something to celebrate. Death is just another experience on the long journey of my life and yours. This is why when you and I celebrate on Easter Sunday morning we sing:

'He lives, He lives! Christ Jesus lives today,
He walks with me, and talks with me
Along life's narrow way
He lives! He lives!
Salvation to impart,
You asked me how I know he lives,
He lives within my heart!'"

Grandpa says, "I do not have all the answers to explain why this is possible, but I do know it is true because it is a self-authenticating truth that lives in my heart."

When a death occurs in Grandpa's family, they celebrate life! Grandpa says, "When my father died, we celebrated life. When my mother died we celebrated life! When my brother died we celebrated life! When my sister died recently we celebrated life! When I die my family will celebrate life! When a loved one dies, we like everyone else, feel sorrow, and the loneliness of the separation, but we do not weep as people without hope, but we celebrate because death is just another experience in life. Death is a part of God's plan. Death is a time for families to celebrate Christ's resurrection and victory over death, in which we share."

Grandpa says, "When I consider all the wonders of God's marvelous grace and what he has done for me I cannot help but respond in gratitude." Grandpa and Grandma understand that giving is central in the celebration of worship. "We love God because he first loved us. Out of his love, God gave his son on the cross. That gift has made possible all of the blessings that we celebrate in worship. How can we do less than give ourselves totally back to him as an expression of gratitude?" Grandpa says, "That means our resources and our money. I hope that God can look at our checkbook and know that we love him by the way we give our possessions that He has given us. We do not have to give in order to be saved, we give because we are celebrating God's great gift of himself, and that as unworthy as we are, we respond by giving of ourselves."

Christianity is never rightly understood until it is seen as a great celebration of gratitude. Grandpa says, "When the plates are passed for our gifts in the worship service, God forbid that we should ever think of it as a collection. It is an expression of our gratefulness to a gracious God who is always giving."

Grandpa says, "My life is motivated and shaped by the experience of worship, it keeps me ticking day after day."

CHAPTER 8
DREAMS DO COME TRUE

Grandpa says, "There was a blueprint of the world in the mind of God before he created it." There is nothing that ever happens by accident. Reality happens first in the mind of God or in the mind of a man. Before there was a man on the moon, there was a Buck Rogers comic strip. Before the discovery of America, Columbus dreamed of a strong new world.

When Grandpa was a small boy, he dreamed all kinds of things that sprang from his imagination. He dreamed up make believe playmates and worlds of fantasy. When he talked about them, his mother would often say, "Son, I don't know what we are going to do with you if you don't quit letting your imagination run off with you. You must quit telling such wild stories." Grandpa would become alarmed and wonder what was wrong with him. However, he just kept dreaming, and his imagination continued to feed his dreams, even to this day. He later discovered that the imagination is one of God's greatest gifts, and is a very important ingredient of creative learning. Grandpa says, "I am very grateful for the gift of imagination."

Grandpa says, "I know that dreams do come true, because they have come true in my own life." When Grandpa was a boy, he dreamed of one day being a fine preacher and caring pastor. He and his old dog, Teddy, used to hike out to Blue Bell island and there in the beautiful sanctuary that God provided, he would conduct moving worship services and preach eloquent sermons. An old log provided the worship center, and Grandpa and Teddy would set-up two branches that formed a cross behind it, against the beautiful green backdrop of the forest. The blue bells became large crowds of people waiting with anticipation. Grandpa imagined they had all kinds of needs, hurts, guilt, frustrations and disappointments in their lives. They needed to be healed by the great physician.

Grandpa had a short stump that was shaped like a pulpit, and he and Teddy had laid a board across it to hold the Bible. Grandpa would announce a hymn and the robins, redbirds, bluebirds and quail sang great anthems with joy and enthusiasm as the trickling water of Three Mile Creek provided an organ accompaniment in the background. Grandpa would then quote words of scripture he had memorized in Sunday School, "Come to me, all that labor and are heavy laden, and I will give you rest. Take my yoke upon you, and learn from me; for I am gentle and lowly in heart, and you will find rest for your souls. For my yoke is easy, and my burden is light." As Grandpa broke the bread of life, God's spirit moved among the people and healed hurts and provided forgiveness. The blue bells stood taller and more beautiful. Teddy, of course, was on the front row with adoring eyes fixed upon Grandpa. At the right times he would nod his head and even dare to "woof" an Amen! Grandpa's heart would burst with joy as he felt he was an instrument through which God spoke his healing message of redeeming love to the waiting hearts. Grandpa says, "It was so real that it had to come true in the future. It took time, hard work, a lot of prayer, but this one thing I know, dreams do come true." Dreams are a part of the stuff that makes Grandpa's life worth living. These dreams are the product of Grandpa's imagination.

Grandpa would listen to Wayne King, "The Waltz King," Guy Lombardo playing the "Sweetest Music this Side of Heaven," or Glen Miller with his inimitable style of "swing." As he listened, he dreamed of the day he would have a band broadcasting and playing in beautiful ballrooms. He would listen to the radio and dream, listen to recordings and dream. He would make the most of every opportunity to hear big name bands in person when they appeared in the area where he lived, and he would dream. He began to act on his dreams and purchased a saxophone and moved closer to the dream. He soon was exploring the possibilities of organizing and recruiting musicians who wanted to play in a dance band. Grandpa says, "Dreams do come true when you put legs on your dreams and move steadily into the future." Grandpa's dream became a reality.

Grandpa says, "Dreams are not an end, but a beginning. A dream is a blueprint of something that I believe will happen in the future if I believe in it so much that I take the first step toward that dream and continue to walk forward until it is a reality." When Grandpa surrendered his life to God and answered the call to ministry, he believed in the blueprint of his dream and began immediately to take the first step of preparation. That was a license to preach and a college education. He continued to move step by step through seminary and ordination. Grandpa says, "You must keep dreaming and add new dreams to the old ones."

In Grandpa's second appointment to three small churches, Salvisa, Clay Lick and Joseph's Chapel, Grandpa and Grandma moved into an old parsonage that had been an old southern style mansion with long white pillars on the front that extended to both floors of the house with porches on both levels. In its day it had been a structure with character and beauty. The problem now was that the pillars were rotten, and the porch was falling down. The stone foundation of the house had given way, and the floors in the house were sagging. Every time it rained you had to put buckets and pans all over the house to catch the water. It had a fireplace in every room, but not one could be used as the bricks and mortar had been allowed to deteriorate and fall into the fireplace and none of them was safe. It had a "path" instead of a "bath." Baths had to be taken in an old fashioned washtub. The list went on and on. Professional architects agreed it was not practical to spend money on a restoration. Grandpa began to dream what seemed to be an unrealistic dream, a new parsonage. One by one, men and women of the church got caught up in Grandpa's dream. Several large gifts of money came from unexpected sources. Two years later a beautiful new modern parsonage was completed. The miracle was that it was paid for when it was completed. That was a part of Grandpa's dream, a blueprint that first sprang from Grandpa's imagination. Grandpa says, "Everything that is worthwhile happens first in the mind of a person. Dreams do come true, and they are the source of all reality."

When Grandpa was a small boy he read all the books he could get his hands on. He read <u>The Swiss Family Robinson</u>, <u>Treasure Island</u>, <u>Tom Sawyer</u> and <u>Huckleberry Finn</u>. The Oliver Hardy series of boys books and countless other books. He would tell everyone that he was going to write a book. Grandpa's mom would say, "Don't talk about it, maybe you will some day, but not now." Grandpa has dreamed about writing a book for as long as he can remember. The dream often got pushed out of the conscious mind, but it kept creeping into the conscious level of Grandpa's mind. It would not go away. Grandpa said to himself, "I am going to write my book." The only problem was he was busy being a pastor, preaching sermons, conducting funerals or weddings. Grandpa says, "One of the real joys of retirement is that you have time to make old dreams come true."

Grandpa was 79 years old when he bought a computer and fell in love with word processing. He had already started writing several chapters of his book in longhand. The computer brought new incentive and motivation. Grandpa spent so much time in front of the monitor that Grandma said, "You're in love with that thing." Grandpa had simply discovered a new tool that could help make his dream of writing a book come true. Grandpa fed the chapters he had written in longhand into the processor. It made it easy to correct errors, move blocks of material, and change sentence structure. The computer is very forgiving and offers one new start after another. Grandpa began to put legs on his dreams, and he was off and running (Not too fast at his age), but running nevertheless.

Grandpa attended two writers seminars at the University of Illinois on the Springfield, Illinois, campus, and really had a ball. Grandpa found he was quite a novelty in the seminars because he was still trying to learn at the age of 80. They could hardly believe Grandpa had taken up the computer at 79 and at 80 was writing a book. It was really fun for Grandpa to participate and sharpen his skills. Grandpa says, "I think the computer is a wonderful tool to enable me to make my dreams come true. I also discovered it is just a dumb machine, and it can do nothing unless I give it a command and tell it what to do." The person who operates a computer is what is special, very special. God has wonderfully made you.

Grandpa says, "It takes a man or woman, that God has made in his own image, with creative imagination to build a computer. A computer is not a miracle, the person who made the computer is the miracle." A computer happened first in the mind of a person, and persons are still masters of technology. Without a person with a creative mind, there would never have been a computer. Grandpa says, "This book happened first in my mind and grew over many years. As I near 81 years of age, I am getting very close to the completion of this book. I am deeply grateful for modern technology and the word processor that enables me to make my dream come true more quickly, more efficiently, and to improve the quality of my writing. It is a high privilege to live in this new day of technology. Dreams do come true. Dear Granddaughter, dreams keep me ticking."

Grandpa says: "An eternal optimist is a person who sees things as they really are, but also sees God at work in everything."

Chapter 9
Eternal Optimist

Grandpa gets up every morning and hits the floor running (not too fast these days). He grabs Grandma and says, "It's really a wonderful day!" Grandma yawns and says, "What's so wonderful about it? I wish you wouldn't talk to me until I get awake. Keep your mouth shut and don't make so much noise." After breakfast Grandpa and Grandma wash and dry the dishes. Grandpa tries again, "Look at that sunshine. This is really a great day!" Grandma says, "You already said that, besides it is probably going to get real hot.

Grandma says, "Grandpa is a cockeyed optimist who never sees things as they really are. He looks at the world through rose colored glasses."

Grandpa immediately disagrees (as usual) and says, "It just ain't so. I am not a cockeyed optimist, I am an eternal optimist, and there is a great deal of difference! An eternal optimist sees things as they really are, recognizing both the good and the bad. Every circumstance has Good News! and Bad News! I can focus on either one I choose!" The following words illustrate this truth:

Two men sat behind prison bars,
One saw mud and the other saw stars!

Grandpa says, "Which man do you want to be like? I choose to look at the stars rather than the mud." An eternal optimist is also conscious of another dimension. God is actively at work in every circumstance of life, both the good and the bad. This makes a difference. Grandpa says, "That is the crux of the whole matter. When you get God into the picture, everything begins to shape up, even the bad. God is actively at work in all the messes man makes. That is the basis for eternal optimism."

Grandpa sites the following grounds for his optimist: first, the Old Testament; secondly, the New Testament; and most important of all, Jesus Christ and His Cross.

Grandpa opens the Old Testament and is greeted with these words, "In the beginning God created the heavens and the earth." This points out God's creative activity. Read on, "And the earth was without form, and void; and darkness was upon the face of the deep..." That's a pretty dark and gloomy picture. Which do you choose to dwell on? Grandpa reads on, "And the Spirit of God moved upon the face of the waters." Here is God's activity, and the picture begins to change. Grandpa sees, "Light" and "Darkness." "Day" and "Night." How different darkness becomes when it is followed by the light of day. When God moves, things change for the better. Things begin to improve. Thanks to God! That is the story found throughout the Old Testament.

Grandpa says, "The Old Testament is a story about men making all kinds of messes, and God steps into the picture and cleans them up. When God gets into the picture, the impossible becomes a possibility."

Grandpa opens the Old Testament to Exodus and finds the story of Moses and the children of Israel at the Red Sea. What does he find? An impossible situation. You know the story. The children of Israel were captives of the Pharaoh in Egypt. Moses hears God speak from a "burning bush," calling him to lead the children of Israel out of bondage! After arguing with God, Moses finally accepts the challenge.

After the plagues are sent upon the Egyptians, the Pharaoh allows Moses and the children of Israel to flee into the wilderness. God is with them every step of the journey. They finally come to the Red Sea, and there is no way to cross. Pharaoh, in the meantime, has a change of heart and takes all the chariots and all the horsemen in Egypt and is hot on their trail. He is bearing down on them. The children of Israel forget how God has taken care of them and complains to Moses about bringing them out here in the wilderness to die. To them, it was a "no win" situation. The Red Sea was on one side, and the Pharaoh and all the chariots and all the horsemen of Egypt pursuing from the other side. Pharaoh was determined to wipe them out! Moses knew how to follow instructions, "And Moses stretched out his hand over the sea; and the Lord caused the sea to go back by a strong east wind all that night. . . And the children of Israel went into the midst of the sea upon dry ground: and the waters were a wall unto them on their right hand, and on their left." (Wow! What an engineering feat that was). Grandpa reads on "And the Egyptians pursued and went in after them." (Lookout! Here comes Moses with that long reach again!). "And the Lord said unto Moses, stretch out thine hand over the sea... And the waters returned, and covered the chariots, and horsemen, and all the hosts of Pharaoh that came into the sea after them, there remained not so much as one of them." That was some feat. God got into the picture, and the impossible became possible. The picture always changes when we become aware of God's activity in our lives.

Grandpa says, "The Old Testament bares witness to the fact that God is one who participates in history, in the daily activities of people like you and me. That makes a difference, and it is why I am an eternal optimist."

The same truth is found throughout the Old Testament. Read the story of Abraham, Gideon, David and Goliath, or Daniel in the fiery furnace or the lion's den. God is always present and active.

Grandpa says, "WOW! Is it ever fun to read the Old Testament. It is an amazing and exciting book. I read it and find Got at work. Where He is at work, there is hope."

Grandpa says, "The New Testament is even more amazing, and I find cause for optimism in every story about Jesus."

Grandpa opens the New Testament and is greeted by the birth of Jesus. "And she shall bring forth a son, and you shall call his name JESUS: for he shall save his people from their sins." There has never been a birth like it, nor shall there ever be. Look at a few facts about that birth:

Born in the small obscure village of Bethlehem
No room in the Inn for his pregnant mother
Laid in the hay with farm animals
No doctors, nurses, or mid-wife
Father was a carpenter
Parents, and God were the only ones present

Grandpa says, "I stand in awe and wonder as I look at a few of the things that happened because of that birth."

Angels sang the announcement of his birth
Shepherds heard and came to worship him
Wise men from the east followed his star
Wise men fell down and worshiped him
Wise men rejoiced, and presented him with gifts
Wise men still worship him and give him gifts
King Herod was afraid and tried to kill him
God broke into history in a personal way
God split history in two
Calendars are marked by his birth—B.C. & A.D.

Grandpa says, "It's an incredible wonder! In every century since his birth, there are men like me who believe He changes and motivates their lives now! Isn't that incredible? Are you surprised I am an optimist?"

Grandpa gets excited as he reads the thrilling stories of Jesus. As Grandpa reads the New Testament, he finds that Jesus makes some incredible statements about himself. In John's Gospel, Grandpa reads these words: "... he that has seen me has seen the Father God." Grandpa says, "WOW! I know what God looks like and how He acts with people like me. Jesus has given me a video of God moving among us. Isn't that something!" John frames the same truth in these words: "And the word (God) was made flesh, and dwelt among us; and we beheld his glory..." Grandpa says, "We have a walking, talking picture of God and all we have to do is look at Jesus and we see and know God." Let's take a look with Grandpa as he guides us on his journey. In the book of Mark, Grandpa reads of how the disciples rebuked the people who brought little children to Jesus. Grandpa reads these words: ". . . and Jesus said unto them, 'Suffer the little children to come unto me, and do not forbid them, for of such is the kingdom of God. . . ' And he took them up in his arms, put his hands upon them, and blessed them." Grandpa exclaims, "Holy smoke! That's God blessing the little children. Isn't that something, God loves little children! God is love. That's something to be optimistic about."

Grandpa continues to read another story in John. A woman was caught in the act of adultery. The Scribes and Pharisees cast her at the feet of Jesus, and say according to the law she should be stoned to death. Jesus kneels and writes in the sand. As they continue to press him, he arises to full stature and says, "He that is without sin among you, let him first cast a stone at her." Jesus stoops again and continues to write in the sand. In shame, all her critics slip away. Jesus lifts his eyes and stands as he says, "...Woman where are your accusers? Has no man condemned you?" She said, "No man, Lord." And Jesus said to her, "Neither do I condemn you; go and sin no more." Grandpa is elated as he says, "What a picture of God! (remember Jesus is a picture of God walking among us). God is forgiveness. Boy! That is really Good News for a guilt-ridden generation made up of people like you and me. God forgives me and points to a better life! That makes Grandpa optimistic!"

Grandpa continues his journey in the New Testament and reads another story about Jesus. In the book of Matthew, Grandpa reads these words: "And as Jesus passed forth from one place to another, he saw a man, named Matthew, sitting at the receipt of custom: and he says unto him: 'Follow me.' And he rose, and followed him." Grandpa asks, "How many men follow you or me simply because we give them an invitation to do so?" This is an intriguing story that tells Grandpa that there is a powerful magnetism in the person of God as pictured by Jesus. God is not the God who we have often pictured in such a way that he turns people off. This is an attractive God that men follow, it's incredible. That is cause for optimism.

Grandpa continues to read excitedly in Matthew's Gospel of a woman who has been sick with a blood disease for 12 years. She crawls through a large crowd, thinking that if she could just touch the hem of the garment of Jesus she would be healed. Jesus saw her and said, "Daughter, be of good comfort; thy faith has made you whole." The scriptures say, "And the woman was made whole." Grandpa says, "Our generation is ever learning, but never coming to the knowledge of truth about the importance of faith in healing. We really need to take a long look at Jesus as he relates to God's inherent process of healing in our lives." In the midst of our diseases, including AIDS, cancer, heart trouble and all the diseases that haunt us, there is cause for optimism found in the picture of God we find in Jesus. He is the master of healing. Where he is at work, there is always cause for optimism. Grandpa says, "God is healing and wholeness. He is by our beds of pain and sickness. He is the author of hope and healing."

Grandpa says, "I am an eternal optimist because in the New Testament I discover that God is love, forgiveness, healing and wholeness. How could I be less than an eternal optimist?"

Grandpa says, "The watershed of all history is found in the Cross of Christ. The Cross is a time exposure of the timeless love of God entering into the sin, suffering, pain, and death of men and women. I stand at the Cross and weep for I know it was for me. I confess I do not know all that means. It is a mystery." The old spiritual lifts up the 64 dollar question, "Were You There When They Crucified My Lord?" Grandpa stands and weeps and says, "I was there when they drove the nails in his hands and feet, when they drove the spear in his side, when they spit in his face, when he bore the scorn. I was there and it was my sin, my burden of guilt, for which he suffered. It was for me. I try to live out my life in gratitude for this amazing gift of grace." Grandpa says, "I am glad God gave us a picture instead of thousands of words of philosophy, christology, or theology, over which men and women fight. I simply cling to the Cross, recognizing it is here that I find forgiveness, mercy, love and wholeness for my fragmented life. Did it make me perfect? No! (I do long to be). One thing I know, I am not what I once was. Grandma and God have made me perfect/almost, and they have made a lot of improvements. I have tried to help as best I could. I glory in the Cross of Christ, and I am filled with gratitude as I face the future with a new personal relationship to God, my neighbor, and the world. I face that future assured I shall never drift beyond his love and care, even in death and beyond the grave and into eternity. I can be no less than an eternal optimist." Grandpa asks a final question of you, dear reader and friend, "Have you discovered the magnetism and meaning of the Cross? Have you discovered an intimate personal relationship with God that brings meaning, purpose and direction to your life? That is the ultimate question for each one of us."

Grandpa concludes, "The Cross is the most significant reason I am an eternal optimist."

When Grandpa was a small boy, God had already given him the gift of optimism. That is why the "Out House" was not a stinking old building out back to be put up with. It was a sanctuary of learning and opportunity that blessed Grandpa's life throughout these many years. It is a gift of God. As Grandma maintained that spiritual gift through the years, and cultivated it, God gave him an even greater Gift through Christ and His Cross. He gave Grandpa the gift of eternal optimism. Grandpa says, "At 80 years of age, I look with joy and anticipation to greater things yet to come from God's good hand of grace. Optimism keeps Grandpa ticking."

Grandpa says: "My heart is always warmed when one of my offspring calls me Grandpa. It shapes and motivates my life."

CHAPTER 10
NAMES THAT CHANGE

Grandpa and his dad stood facing each other and were in a serious conversation as Grandpa and his family prepared to return home to Kentucky after a short Christmas visit during Grandpa's college days. Neither of them knew it would be the last time they would ever see each other again (Grandpa's dad died a few months later of a sudden heart attack). Grandpa's dad said, "Son, I always planned for you to be here to take over my building business when I die, I really miss your not being here. However, your being called to the ministry is what is really important. It is not what I want, but what God has planned for you. I understand and support you all the way." When Grandpa's dad called Grandpa "Son," it communicated much more than one might imagine. It was always said with pride, respect, and conveyed deep expectations that a father had for his son. Grandpa's life is still motivated by the way his dad said, "Son." Grandpa says, "I can still hear him calling me 'Son,' and I strive to be a better person, to accomplish more worthwhile things, and to meet the expectations he had for me. The name 'Son' has shaped and motivated my life."

Grandpa often calls people he respects "Son." Grandpa calls his own boys, "Son" and hopes some day it will mean as much to them as the name does to him. He not only called his boys by that name, but other persons who are friends and co-workers as well. While serving as a District Superintendent and a member of the Bishop's Cabinet in the Central Illinois Conference, Grandpa called the Bishop, "Son" (during a cabinet session). All the superintendents and the Bishop broke into laughter. Grandpa did not do this out of disrespect, but it flowed naturally from the depths of his being as the highest name of respect of which he could think. "Son" is the epitome of complements in Grandpa's vocabulary. Grandpa says, "What people call us is highly significant and motivates our thoughts and actions."

Jesus knew that names and titles make a difference when he changed Simon's name to Peter. Jesus said unto him, "Thou art Peter, and upon this rock I will build my church..." Jesus tied the new name to great expectations, and Peter was forever different. The same thing happened to Saul of Tarsus, a persecutor of the early Christians. Saul was converted on the road to Damascus and became known as Paul. Paul became a great preacher and missionary and wrote a large portion of the New Testament.

Grandpa has been given many different names and titles that have made a difference in his daily life. Sometimes they were not all positive. Names can be "Good News" or "Bad News." Grandpa says, "When I was called by a bad name, I tried not to respond in a negative way and to learn from the experience. When they were good names, I tried to be worthy."

Grandpa received an appointment to three rural churches in Kentucky: Salvisa, Clay Lick, and Joseph's Chapel. There were many good folks in these churches, and they all called Grandpa, "Brother." They said it with respect, dignity, and love. They made Grandpa and his family feel that they were a part of their family and the family of God by the way they used this endearing term. To this day, Grandpa can remember how some of these wonderful people called him, "Brother." It made a difference in how Grandpa worked with people. Grandpa says, "Thanks, to those kind and gracious people who taught me so much about relationships."

Grandpa received a Bachelor of Arts degree from Asbury College. He was then called a college graduate, and it sounded good to Grandpa because it was a fulfillment of one step toward his dream of becoming an ordained minister. This gave Grandpa confidence that he could still learn after being out of school for 12 years. Grandpa received a Master of Divinity degree from Garrett Evangelical Seminary. He had another new name. He was a seminary graduate. On the 21st day of May, 1972, MacMurray College bestowed a Doctor of Divinity degree on Grandpa and once again he received another new name. He was called "Doctor." Like most people, Grandpa was human enough to be proud of these accomplishments. All of these educational titles were significant and helped to shape Grandpa's life. However, Grandpa was able to get them into proper perspective and now he is quick to say,

In my hand no degree I bring,
Simply to Thy cross I cling!

Grandpa says, "I have tried to be worthy of each new name I have received and am grateful to God who called me to serve people in the ministry of Jesus Christ."

The church has also given Grandpa names that have shaped his life along the journey. In September of 1945 Grandpa was given his first local preacher's license by St. Luke Methodist Church in Louisville. For the next few years, he was called a local preacher while attending college. Grandpa was glad to have this new name. On August 21, 1952, Grandpa was ordained a Deacon of the Kentucky Annual Conference at Morehead, Kentucky. Grandpa was now called a Deacon. Grandpa says, "Old Peter was lucky to only have one new name. I have been given so many new names that I can't remember them all." Grandpa tried to wear these names with humility. Grandpa was ordained an Elder in the Illinois Conference on June 12, 1955. Grandpa was now called an Elder in full connection in the Illinois Conference. Grandpa says, "Wow! These names just keep coming." Sometimes Grandma wondered who she married. Perplexing, to say the least. However, she faithfully walked every step of the journey, though sometimes it was very difficult." Even Grandpa wondered at times who he was. Grandpa says, "It is only by the grace of God and Grandma that I am able to keep my head on my shoulders and remember who I am."

Grandpa also received another new name when the Bishop chose him to be a member of his cabinet and named him the Decatur District Superintendent. Grandpa was glad to be a District superintendent and endeavored to be a pastor of all of the ministers and their families who served in his district. The needs of pastors and their families are far greater than meets the eye. Their problems are often magnified by the many unreasonable expectations of congregations and public scrutiny. Grandpa felt these were six years of his most fruitful and satisfying ministry.

The Rushville community, where Grandpa has lived in retirement for more than 16 years, has contributed to the growing list of names by which he has been called. Grandpa says, "Can you believe there are more names to come? Of course, it isn't everybody who lives to be as old as Grandpa."

Grandpa was named the Grand Marshall of the 1992 Smiles Day Parade in recognition of his many years of service to the Rushville Community. It was especially meaningful to Grandpa, since it followed his open heart surgery.

It gave Grandpa a much needed emotional lift at a down period in his life. Grandpa says, "At that time, I was six inches below the bottom. I was having trouble trying to reach up to the bottom." When you're that far down, you will grab any hand that reaches in to help you up." Grandpa says, "It is a humbling experience when an entire community joins together to say, 'Thank you.'" It was a great day for Grandpa and Grandma as they rode in the back of a red convertible leading the parade along the route from the Schuyler County fairgrounds to the park in the city square where the celebration has been held for many years. Grandpa says, "I love Smiles Day. I believe smiling helps us to get our troubles into proper perspective and enables us to live with them." However, Grandpa felt guilty when he thought of Christ riding on the back of an ass on Palm Sunday. Grandpa prayed, "Dear Lord, forgive us for being so human and in our glorying in the praise of men."

Grandpa has been an active Rotarian for many years. Grandpa believes in the purpose of Rotary as expressed in its motto, "Service Above Self." This motto is compatible with the teachings of Jesus, who said, "He who would become great among you, let him become the servant of all, for the son of man did not come to be served, but to serve and give his life as a ransom." The Rushville Rotary Club named Grandpa "Rotarian of the Year" in 1995, and the club made him a "Paul Harris Fellow" in 1994. Grandpa feels this is important because fellow Rotarians gave a $1,000.00 gift to Rotary International foundation that is striving to eradicate polio by giving vaccine to children in all of the under-developed countries in the world. The Foundation also seeks to provide scholarships for the Student Exchange program, and many other worthy causes in pursuit of world understanding and peace. Grandpa wears this award with gratitude and is glad for the work that is being accomplished by the Rotary International Foundation. Every Friday morning, Grandpa sits down at his word processor and writes a column called "Rotary Reaches Out" for the <u>Rushville Times</u>. It is an avenue of expression that brings satisfaction to Grandpa.

Grandpa is striving to wear the name that Rotary has given to him by putting "Service Above Self" in his daily life. Grandpa says, "This is not easy because I, like everyone else, struggle with my own selfish egotism. By God's gift of grace, I try to reach the ideal. If you think it is easy to do, I dare you to try putting 'Service Above Self' for six months."

Grandpa was named "Pastor Emeritus" by First United Methodist Church of Rushville, Illinois, on September 8, 1996. This is another new name that gives Grandpa a warm and fuzzy feeling. He feels proud, but unworthy. Grandpa has always loved this church and felt it was one of the great county seat community churches in the conference and in all of Methodism. Grandpa says, "I shall forever cherish this new name by being the best witness possible for Christ and the church for the remaining years of my life."

Grandpa says, "I try to keep all honors, degrees, and names in perspective. I remember what a wise old saint said, 'Honors and degrees are like roses, they are to be sniffed and not digested!'"

Several years ago Grandpa dressed up in a rabbit suit that covered his entire body, his head, and he wore long white ears. He wore dark glasses over his eyes. Grandpa looked like a huge white rabbit and was a sight to behold! He walked a few doors down the street to the home of a grandson where a pre-Easter party for kids was in full swing. A number of Grandpa's great-grandkids were present. Grandpa immediately became the center of attention. A chair was placed on the deck for Grandpa, and he took the little kids on his lap and gave them Easter eggs.

Grandpa and the kids had a ball visiting and sharing rabbit talk (Grandpa even had a few mothers sitting on his lap). None of his great-grandchildren knew him. As Grandpa was leaving, one of his little great-granddaughters came up and whispered in his ear. "I know who you are, but I haven't told anyone." Then she said, "You're my Grandpa." Grandpa's heart filled with pride and joy. He shed a few tears. Grandpa was reminded that the most important values of life are relationships and that the most important name for him at the present time is "Grandpa." Wow! What a high privilege. Grandpa says, "This is the highest and most sacred name I could be given. It is truly a wonderful privilege to be called 'Grandpa' by nine grandchildren, and nine great-grandchildren."

Grandpa recently read in an Ann Lander's column of a man who was ashamed for persons in his office to find out he was a grandpa. What a sad situation. Grandpa says, "I am glad I know who I am, I am Grandpa!" That is the reason for the title of this book. Grandpa hopes God will say, "He was a good Grandpa."

Grandpa says, "My grandchildren and great-grandchildren are still shaping and motivating my life, they keep me ticking."

Grandpa says, "The three names that are most significant in defining who I really am, are SON, BROTHER, AND GRANDPA. My dear granddaughter, relationships are the most important values in my life, my relationship to God, my family and the family of God."

Chapter 11
Grandpa's Love Affair!

Grandpa fell head over heels in love during the early years of his pastorate in the Rushville Church (please don't tell Grandma). It was a long time affair that he never got over. Grandpa fell in love with Culbertson Memorial Hospital. He spent many hours there visiting patients and their families. A great many things have happened to deepen this relationship over a long period of time. Grandpa developed a strong bond of friendship with the administration, doctors and the staff. Some of those relationships have become life time friendships.

One Saturday evening Grandpa was enjoying a night at home and was preparing for the Sunday morning worship services. It happened to be the weekend of the local high school prom. Grandpa received a telephone call from the Schuyler County Sheriff's office. There had been a bad wreck on Highway 24 near the Schuyler/Fulton County line. A car coming down the steep hill had gotten out of control and hit an abutment. Two ambulances were on the way to Culbertson Hospital with four persons critically injured. The Sheriff had requested that Grandpa meet them at the hospital on arrival. Grandpa jumped into his car and was at the hospital in a matter of minutes and was there before the ambulance arrived. This turned out to be a hectic night. One 15 year old girl was pronounced dead on arrival at the hospital. Another 16 year old girl was in very critical condition, and the two men were both critical. The two married men from Pekin, Illinois, had picked up the girls on the street. One of the girls had left home to go to a drug store to pick up a prescription for her mother. The four persons had been drinking and were traveling at a high rate of speed when the accident occurred. One man's leg was completely severed and found later. Culbertson Hospital was short-staffed with only one local doctor, and a surgeon from Macomb, available. Grandpa was pressed into duty. They placed a surgical gown, cap, mask and surgical gloves on him. He worked side by side with the doctors and the nurse throughout the night (This could not happen today). At approximately 1:30 a.m. he was called out of the operating room to inform the mother that her daughter was dead. She had no knowledge where her daughter was, from the time she left home to get a prescription, until she was informed that her daughter had been in an accident, and she was told to go to Culbertson Hospital in Rushville. Grandpa returned to the operating room where he worked until 4:30 a.m. He finally got to bed at 5:15 a.m., and was up at 7:00 a.m., and preached in two worship services at First Methodist Church that Sunday morning. Grandpa says: "I felt a warm affection for those two doctors, the nurse, and Culbertson hospital. That affection has continued to grow over the years."

There were many experiences over the years that deepened Grandpa's on-going love affair with Culbertson hospital. In 1978 Grandpa's son-in-law was injured late one evening in a farm accident that nearly took his life. He had a serious brain injury and was taken to the emergency room of Culbertson Memorial Hospital. He was given treatment that stabilized his condition and made it possible for him to be transferred to Springfield Memorial Hospital where he received intensive brain surgery. The emergency treatment that he received at Culbertson saved his life, and he is alive and well today.

Grandpa says, "I have learned that Culbertson hospital is a caring institution, and fate has made it an integral part of my life. My love for this small rural hospital continues to grow through the years."

When Grandpa decided to retire from the active ministry in 1982 at the age of 67, it seemed that the providence of God led to Rushville, and Culbertson Hospital. Grandpa and Grandma had three married children in Rushville and the surrounding area. A daughter was the postmistress at Littleton, Illinois, only nine miles north of Rushville. Son one was on the staff of Western Illinois University in Macomb, Illinois, just 28 miles north, and son two was on the staff of FS (Farm Supply) in Rushville. Three grandchildren and their families were located in Rushville. In addition to the family incentive, was Culbertson Memorial Hospital. Culbertson was in a life or death financial struggle for survival (due to the many changes in government health care policies and procedures). During that period of time, many rural hospitals were forced out of business in nearby communities. Small hospitals were closed all over the nation. Grandpa was given an invitation to join the staff at Culbertson Hospital, by a long time friend who was Chairman of the Board of Trustees. Grandpa was to work in the area of public relations and fund raising.

Grandpa immediately began work on a five year plan, setting up a full time Development and Public Relations Department. Grandpa became the Director of the Department. He developed a mailing list that included thousands of names and addresses, not only of people in the local community, but absentee landowners, and people who had any kind of relationship to the Rushville community that lived elsewhere. He selected the appropriate slogan or motto "Culbertson Cares." This was on every piece of publicity and any printed material that went out of the hospital. Grandpa knew from personal experience that Culbertson Memorial Hospital's staff and employees did care. He wrote a weekly news column for the <u>Rushville Times</u> under the byline "Culbertson Cares." Grandpa soon became known as "Mr. Culbertson Cares." Sometimes while visiting in other nearby communities, someone would come up and say, "I know you, you're 'Mr. Culbertson Cares.'" These articles always contained personal, down-home items written to make people conscious that Culbertson Memorial Hospital truly did care about people. Grandpa started a short radio program, on Radio Station WKXQ, known as "Culbertson Shares." Grandpa interviewed doctors, staff, administration, nurses, candy strippers and happy patients who felt grateful for the care they had received. Grandpa was always seeking to make people conscious of the one thing that Culbertson had to offer, caring personal service. Grandpa spoke to many civic groups both in the local community and in the surrounding towns. He had one theme, "Culbertson Cares." Grandpa started a quarterly newspaper known as <u>AWARE</u>. This was mailed to people on the mailing list. It recognized and expressed appreciation for every gift large or small during the past quarter. Money was soon coming in from local citizens and from persons from California to New Jersey, and Florida to Wisconsin. Grandpa started an "Annual Appeal" that purchased much needed equipment and such things as a van with a lift for transporting residents in the Long Term Care facility and other persons in the community for medical treatment at the hospital. This job was a challenge that let Grandpa express some of the affection he felt in his heart for Culbertson hospital. That "Annual Appeal" is still bringing in thousands of dollars each year for needed equipment replacement and for new modern equipment. A young woman Grandpa trained is now the Director of Development and is doing an excellent job of promoting the "Annual Appeal." Grandpa's love affair with Culbertson Memorial Hospital was very fulfilling and meaningful.

During the ten years Grandpa served as the Director of Development, one of the major goals was to recruit new, young doctors. There was a need for a new Medical Arts Building to house new, modern doctors' offices. The hospital had some funds from estates and other sources. The trustees were reluctant to go in debt for the new building, considering their struggling financial condition. Grandpa said, "Don't get in debt. Let's have a major fund raising campaign and raise the money we need before we start." A number of the board members and the administration did not think it was possible to raise the needed funds. Grandpa said, "Let's try. I think we can do it." Finally, the board approved a campaign and set a goal. Grandpa outlined an eight month campaign designed to raise the needed funds. The campaign was a tremendous success, and the campaign went over the goal. Grandpa helped purchase property needed for the building and parking. When the building was completed in 1986, it was dedicated absolutely debt free. It has been one of the elements that has made Culbertson Hospital one of the small rural hospitals in America that has survived that period, and is now a viable institution operating in the black each month. The hospital has eight doctors on the staff, which is rather amazing for a community of 3500 people. It has a prosperous Outpatient Clinic with specialists from Springfield, Peoria, Quincy, and other surrounding cities in practically every medical specialty. This gives local citizens access to specialists without the added expense of travel to larger cities. The future is bright.

Grandpa says, "My love affair with Culbertson Memorial Hospital has been fulfilling and meaningful (by the way, I now live in a new home that is located on the property that was the former site of Dr. Culbertson's old home place). My life seems to be providentially connected with Culbertson."

CHAPTER 12
PAIN AND PEACE

One day Grandpa met Artie under unusual circumstances. Artie quickly told Grandpa he wanted to be friends. There was something about Artie that Grandpa didn't like. He seemed to be so darned insistent and stubborn. Artie kept insisting that he was going to be Grandpa's constant companion for the rest of his life. Grandpa thought that if he was, it was going to be pure hell (Grandma didn't like Artie either). Artie stubbornly kept telling Grandpa that he was going to be Grandpa's constant companion and that Grandpa might as well accept him and make peace. Grandpa never told anyone about Artie (he suffered in silence) and kept hoping that he would go away and leave him alone, but it never happened. Grandpa was 65 years of age when he met Artie, and that relationship has lasted for 15 years even though Grandpa constantly tried in every way possible to break off the relationship. Artie has been as good as his word and has dogged Grandpa's every step since he first met him. There are times Grandpa can hardly stand Artie. It has been a painful experience for Grandpa, but he has finally accepted the fact that Artie is a fellow traveler on his journey. Grandpa still has a tremendous dislike for Artie.

Grandpa lived a virtually pain-free life until he was 65 years of age. Grandpa had excellent health, took very little medicine (not even aspirin), and had never missed a Sunday from the pulpit because of health. His only health problem had been a slight high blood pressure for which he took a small amount of medication. At 65 things began to change. He went to his family physician because of pain in his back. After an examination and several tests, the doctor said, "You have arthritis of the spine. You are going to have more trouble in the future." That was Grandpa's first formal introduction to Artie. Grandpa says, "I can never remember a single pain-free day since that time." Grandpa has learned that pain is a great teacher. Grandpa says it in a few words of verse that follow:

> I walked for days with pleasure
> and I never learned a thing.
> I walked today with pain
> and I'll never be the same.

Pain and suffering are not in vain if we live with it and learn. Artie was only the beginning of Grandpa's experience with pain.

Grandpa suffered a heart failure in 1986. Grandpa and Grandma were vacationing at their condo in Hollywood, Florida. Grandpa went into heart failure and did not know it. He knew he was terribly sick and something was wrong but was not aware that it was heart failure. All Grandpa could think about was getting home. He and Grandma made a decision to sell their condo and did so before leaving Florida. Grandpa drove the more than 1400 miles home, though he was in pain and distress. Grandma usually shared the driving, but Grandpa was uptight and insisted on driving the entire distance. He was in a stupor. They finally arrived in Rushville late in the afternoon, and Grandpa would not go to the doctor until they had unloaded and put everything away. He waited until the next morning. A close friend took him to Culbertson

Hospital. Nothing ever looked better to Grandpa than Culbertson Hospital did that morning. He met his long time friend and physician who took one look at Grandpa and felt his lower legs, and excitedly said, "You are in acute heart failure." Things really began to happen. He called a nurse, and in a matter of moments Grandpa was in the emergency room where they took large amounts of fluid from his body. Grandpa had by then lost consciousness. Grandpa awakened the next day feeling like a new man. Grandpa had not realized how much pressure and pain he had been in for several weeks until after relief had come. Artie was still hanging around trying to get in the last word, but so was the gift of God's peace deep in Grandpa's heart. It was only by the grace of God that Grandpa had not died while in Florida or on the way home. The doctor could not believe that Grandpa drove all the way home in his condition.

Grandpa was learning that he had another companion who walked at his side, and sometimes carried him. His name was Jesus, who Grandpa had known for many years now. Through all this turmoil, Grandpa was not afraid. He felt a deep, abiding peace in his heart which he did not deserve. It was a gift of a merciful God. Grandpa says, "I was finally beginning to learn that pain has no power over God's gift of peace. Pain and peace can live side by side in my life, and the greatest of the two is God's gift of peace. I was also learning that Culbertson hospital truly cares."

Something very wonderful and uplifting happened during all this time of testing. Grandpa and Grandma's 50th wedding anniversary was on March 22, 1986, and the celebration had to be delayed for a month. About a week after Grandpa got out of the hospital, he and Grandma were able to celebrate and greet friends at First United Methodist Church in Rushville. They did so against the doctor's better judgment. Grandpa sat on a kitchen stool and shook hands with more than 500 persons from many of their former churches, as well as local folks who came to greet them. It was a joyful occasion with their four children acting as hosts. Grandpa's dear friend, the good doctor, was there throughout the entire time just in case Grandpa went into heart failure and fell off the stool. Artie was there to get in his 'two cents worth,' as usual, but Grandpa's constant companion, the gift of peace was always there. Grandpa says, "I was learning from the great teacher a little bit about patience and perseverance. It was important to do so, for there was more pain to come."

Prior to his heart failure in 1986, Grandpa and Artie met another intruder in the form of hives. This was in 1981. Grandpa began to itch and found a rash on his arms and hands that nearly drove him wild. It spread to his face, in the hair, and other parts of his body (in fact, most other parts). It was accompanied by swelling and it was the most uncomfortable thing Grandpa had ever experienced. It was, in fact, a pain in the b - - - (preachers shouldn't say that word). The doctor called in all kinds of specialists, including a dermatologist, trying to find out what was causing the hives. They could find nothing. Grandpa finally wound up in the Decatur Memorial Hospital for ten days. Grandpa was x-rayed, scanned and given allergy testing. You name it, Grandpa had it. This was all to no avail. Grandpa was given prednisone and aspirin. This helped but was not a cure. Grandpa hated to take prednisone because of the side-effects. Grandpa, Artie and the hives remained suffering companions (all Grandpa could think of was "Misery loves company"). During all this time Grandpa remained productive and served as the Executive Director of Wesley Towers until 1982 and as the Director of Development and Public Relations at Culbertson Hospital in Rushville until 1992. He learned not only to live with pain, but to smile, continue working, and loving people. God's gift of peace was a light that shone into Grandpa's heart. Sometimes when Grandpa couldn't see it, he believed in it anyway. Grandma never missed a single mile in the journey. She was there to love and support Grandpa.

In the meantime Grandpa had a visit to Mayo Brothers Clinic for a complete physical examination. Grandpa took every kind of conceivable test. He swallowed tubes, stood on his head for an x-ray, had brain scans, body scans, was poked in the rear with a tube that ran up his intestines until he thought it was going to come out his throat. Grandpa was finally told that the prednisone and aspirin were the two guilty culprits. He was given other dietary restrictions that he followed religiously for the next few years. When he got back home, Grandpa was a little better, but Artie and the hives were still constantly with him. There was pain without end. God's gift of peace and Grandma's support were the source of strength that made it possible for Grandpa to "hang in there. Grandpa worked, sang, smiled, and learned to accept and live with pain. Patience and perseverance came hard to Grandpa.

There is always a silver lining in every cloud. When Grandpa had his heart failure in 1986, for some unknown reason to the doctors, the hives gave up the ghost and no longer haunted Grandpa's trail. Grandpa says, "Thank God for small favors. One down and one to go. Artie was still there, as persistent as ever."

In 1991 Grandpa's back became so bad that he was about to lose the use of his right leg. After many tests by several different specialists, Grandpa was informed that he must have a spinaldectomy if he was going to continue to walk. A young, skilled neurological surgeon performed the surgery. They were quite concerned about Grandpa's heart, and a cardiologist stood by during the surgery. The surgery was a success, and Grandpa's use of his right leg was restored. The surgeon, however, had told Grandpa that his surgical procedure would not help with his arthritis. He was quite concerned of the arthritic condition of Grandpa's back. You guessed right, old Artie was back and was more persistent than ever. Grandpa was learning how to live with pain. He learned it isn't easy. Grandpa's job was to keep up his work at Culbertson Hospital and enjoy the success he was having in helping to keep funds rolling in that helped make the hospital a viable institution. Artie was also working hard, and there was more pain to come.

On Father's Day, 1992, Grandpa started out walking from his home to the First Christian Church where he was to speak in the morning worship service. Grandma was to come later with other members of the family. This was a distance of only two blocks, but when Grandpa arrived, he was literally gasping for breath. He sat down, and his breathing seemed to improve. He had no pain in the chest area. Shortly before the worship service began, he asked a friend, who was the sheriff, if he would drive him home. Grandpa thought he had indigestion and that a dose of Mylanta would help. Grandpa's son had followed them to the house in his car. Grandpa was suddenly very short of breath again. He asked Son One to take him to Culbertson Hospital Emergency Room. When they entered the hospital, they were greeted warmly by a nurse who was Grandpa's friend. Grandpa blurted out, "I'm in trouble." He immediately became unconscious. In a few minutes he was in the emergency room surrounded with persons who care. In his semiconscious state, he thought of how wonderful it was to be in a place where he had raised the funds to buy much of the fine equipment that was available to give the care he needed.

Grandpa heard his doctor friend of many years say, "I am not sure he is going to make it. He is in severe congestive heart failure." This did not frighten Grandpa. He had peace in his heart and was in the hands of skilled doctors, nurses and technicians with the latest equipment. They put him on oxygen immediately and began removing large amounts of fluid from his body. They were working with the latest technology and drugs that were available.

For some time, Grandpa though he might worship at the great white throne rather than with the good folks at First Christian Church. Grandpa knew it was possible he could slip away from his wonderful family that waited anxiously just outside the emergency room. Grandpa heard his good doctor say, "He is going to make it." He went out to share the "Good News" with Grandpa's waiting family.

In about one hour the struggle was over, and Grandpa was on his way to Memorial Hospital in Springfield in a new modern ambulance with excellent life support equipment. There was a skilled paramedic and a good driver. Through the whole life threatening experience, there was the constant abiding peace. He was not even aware of Artie. Grandma rode in the ambulance and held Grandpa's hand. Hold on tight for there is more pain to come.

Grandpa was to spend more than three weeks in Springfield Memorial Hospital. His cardiologist was one of God's good guys, and he and Grandpa became fast friends. Grandpa was fed intravenously, hooked to a heart monitor, a catheter and much more. Grandpa began to name the equipment they used on him. The intravenous feeder was called "Junior," the heart monitor was the "Eye in the Sky," the bed pan was named "John Sr.," and the catheter was named "The Drip." This tickled the nurses and technicians when Grandpa used these names, and they began to have fun. Grandpa named the nurses and technicians, "God's good gals." He named the doctors and male nurses, "God's good guys." Though Grandpa went through the three most difficult weeks in his life, he really enjoyed his stay at Memorial Hospital in Springfield. Hospitals can be fun!

On July 7, 1992, during that stay, Grandpa had "Open Heart Surgery." The main aortic valve was replaced with a pig valve. Now every time Grandpa passes a pig confinement, he bows and reverently says, "Oink, oink," (Thank you). Grandpa had a wonderful young heart surgeon who Grandpa now calls a "friend." All the doctors who cared for Grandpa were skilled, caring, down-to-earth folks. Grandpa nearly died after surgery with a blocked bowel and an enlarged prostate gland. It extended his hospital stay by several weeks. When Grandpa was able to go home, his recovery was slow. Artie was still with him, and during the weeks in bed he took advantage of Grandpa since he could not work at his exercise program as usual. Grandpa was finally forced to retire from Culbertson hospital during that year due to his limitations. Be prepared, there is more pain to come.

During the period that followed, Grandpa had cataract surgery with intraocular lens implants in both eyes. This was relatively painless, but nerve-wracking. Grandpa came through with good vision after a second laser surgery on both eyes. It was just another little experience with pain, and you guessed right, Ole Artie was really giving Grandpa fits all the way, but his other companion, the gift of peace, was even more faithful, and so was Grandma.

In May of 1993 Grandpa received another blow that almost floored him. He had a growth removed from the right side of his neck as large as a "hens egg." About one week later he came to the house with a large string of fish for supper. Grandma was waiting for him, and he knew something was wrong. The surgeon had called to say the growth was a malignant lymphoma tumor. Grandpa was to see an oncologist. At first, there was unbelief. Grandpa was numb. Why me? But Grandpa thought of how God has been teaching him for a long period of time for this very moment. He accepted the fact and decided he would live as long and as well as he possibly could with God's help. The surgeon made an appointment for Grandpa with an oncologist. Grandpa was informed that his growth was high grade and fast growing in nature, and that he possibly had six months to live. Radiation and chemotherapy were ruled out by a consultation of cancer specialists, because of Grandpa's age, having had five major surgeries in less than five years, his porcine aortic valve, and other medical conditions. The prognosis was discouraging. Grandpa has remained under the care of the oncologist since that time. The first six months Grandpa visited the oncologist monthly for blood analysis, x-rays and a CAT scan at the end of six months. Then the appointments were lengthened to two months. A year passed and the oncologist was amazed. He said, "I don't understand what is happening. If we had given you chemo or radiation, we would have said that is the reason." Grandpa asked, "Am I in remission?" The doctor said, "I don't think so, you are in limbo. In other words I don't know where you are. What have you been doing? How do you explain it?" Grandpa said, "I only know that I have had peace in my heart and I have not been afraid. I do not deserve the gift of peace. It is a gift of God." The doctor replied, "I don't understand that. But whatever it is, it has been working." Nearly four years later, Grandpa is still in limbo and is very much alive. Grandpa is still under the care of the puzzled specialist.

This is how Grandpa explains what has happened. Grandpa claims no great miracle of healing. Grandpa is very much aware that he has cancer and it could become active at any time and take his life.

Prayer is key. Hundreds of people have prayed for Grandpa over the past five years. Evidently God has heard and answered these prayers. Remember, prayer changes things.

Grandpa has learned that CANCER IS NOT A DEATH SENTENCE. IT IS A CALL TO LIFE: It is a call to live "One day at a time." Shortly after Grandpa had heart surgery, Grandma gave him a key chain with a small gold plate attached to it on which were etched these words, "One day at a time." Grandpa decided that these were words of wisdom by which he would live. Grandpa accepts each day as a gift of God's grace. Grandpa says, "I have lived over the average life expectancy for men. Each day is a bonus. I strive to live out of gratitude."

Grandpa has learned that cancer is a call to live a useful life. Grandpa has learned to accept his limitations (the hardest thing to accept is being deaf in one ear and he can't hear out of the other), but to also understand that he must do the things he can. Grandpa discovered that he can do many worthwhile things. Grandpa made a decision to do several things daily. First, he does something good for Grandma. He washes or dries the dishes (sometimes both). He runs the sweeper (he still rebels at dusting). Doing little things for the person we love has the power to heal. Second, Grandpa intentionally does something good each day for one other person outside the family. Grandpa sends a note or a memorial gift in times of death and sorrow, makes a short visit, gives away a smile or passes a compliment. Grandpa holds a door or extends a warm handshake. There are little things that you can do every day for someone outside your family if you become sensitive to people. Third, Grandpa tries to do something good each day for his community and church. It may be a small thing. Grandpa writes a newspaper column each week, gives a check to a worthy cause, lends his influence to worthwhile projects. Grandpa makes telephone calls to the sick, prays for the sick, the pastor and the church. Grandpa prays daily for every member of his family by name. Grandpa says, "This keeps one eighty year old kid busy and makes living with cancer very meaningful and extends life 'One day at a time.' It adds quality living to my years. I plan to live to be a hundred years of age or die trying. I very seldom think of having cancer. Artie, the arthritis, bothers me a whole lot more than the cancer.

Cancer is a call to live with music. There is healing in music. Grandpa and Grandma have a tape player between their twin beds (It's easy to get from one to the other). Every night before going to sleep they listen to good music. They listen to everything from Guy Lombardo (romantic) to symphonies that run the gamut of human emotions. Grandpa says, "Music is food for the soul and brings healing to the human body. No person lives well without God's great gift of music. I am grateful for the way it has brought healing to my body, mind and spirit. You guessed right. Ole Artie is still there."

Grandpa and Grandma had a wonderful surprise last night. Son Four came for an overnight visit. Grandpa was reminded that cancer is a call to live with a greater appreciation for those who love us. This morning, Grandpa and Grandma received a call from Culbertson Hospital informing them that they were great-grandparents for the ninth time. They have a beautiful girl with black hair to light up their lives. WOW! IS LIFE WORTH LIVING! The writer of Proverbs records, "An old man's grandchildren are his glory. . ." Grandpa says, "He is so right if he will include the kids, and great-grandchildren."

Grandpa is planning to live his life, "One day at a time," just as long as he can in a meaningful way. He does not buy the idea that cancer is a death sentence. Grandpa says, "I have lived four years with cancer, and they have been the most meaningful and happy years of my life, in spite of Ole Artie."

Grandpa concludes, "I have been learning about the mystery of pain from the greatest of all teachers, Jesus Christ and his Cross. It sheds its light on my journey through life, and that includes pain. I have found in my personal experience that though pain and peace seem to be contradictory to each other, they can abide together in the same heart and mind and form a whole truth. Patience and perseverance are the fruits of our experience of pain. I wish I understood more fully the mystery of pain, and could express it's meaning more clearly. I do not like pain, in fact, I abhor it, I accept it, and recognize it shapes my life and keeps me ticking! Thanks to God!"

CHAPTER 13

DEATH, DYING, THE FUTURE

Grandpa is quite conscious of his mortality. He is aware that God has not forgotten his address and at some time in the future, God will knock at the door and Grandpa will experience death. Talking about this is not morbid, it is simply facing a fact on the journey of life. All people are dying and will experience death. No field of learning can deny this fact.

Because of Grandpa's experience of God's grace and mercy during his long journey over the past eighty years, it is impossible for him to separate death and dying from God and the future. God is at the beginning of Grandpa's journey. God has accompanied each step he has traveled. God will surely be at the end of the journey and in the future. Grandpa has a good imagination, but he cannot imagine death or the future beyond the grave without God. Grandpa says, "I believe in the future. Death is another experience with God along the journey of life. The future is just another expression of his love and grace that we have discovered in Christ Jesus our Lord."

Grandpa says, "As I move closer to death, I am standing on the edge of newness. WOW! What an exciting adventure that will be."

156

Death is a mystery! Grandpa would be the first to admit that he has many unanswered questions about death. Grandpa never understands the death of a newborn baby, and he gropes for understanding when a youth is suddenly taken by death. Who would be bold enough to try to explain why a young mother or father is taken from an adolescent child or teenage youth who need them so badly. These are times when we do not have the answers. Rest assured, we do not find these answers in any other field of knowledge. We must trust in God. Grandpa says, "I believe in the sun when it refuses to shine. I know it is out there somewhere behind the clouds. I know it will shine again and bring warmth and life to me. I also believe in God's great mercy and love when I cannot understand, and in time he will validate my faith with comfort, love, hope and meaning."

Grandpa believes dying is a process. As we journey through life, our physical bodies wear out and they are no longer a fit place for our spirits to dwell. Death is a friend who releases us from the pain and limitations that growing old brings to our worn out bodies.

Grandpa has written a few words of simple verse that express this truth in a humorous way:

My hair is getting thinner
and my hearing is awfully bad.
If it wasn't all so funny
Grandpa says, "t'would really be sad."

All day long my back is aching
My arms and legs do too,
If it wasn't for God and Grandma
I don't know what I'd do.

In my neck I have this cancer,
malignant lymphoma for sure,

Six months to live, says the doctor
At your age that's all, no cure!

"One day at a time," says Grandma
Grandpa says, "It's a call to live,"
People's prayers, God, and optimism,
Four more years to Grandpa give!

The doctor's perplexed and wonders,
what the heck is taking place.
"A peace that passeth understanding."
To Grandpa, a gift of God's grace!

Grandpa makes the most of each moment.
This book he has written and more,
Each day he does something good for Grandma,
others, community, the church for sure!

God surely knows Grandpa's address
and when the body can take no more,
Standing on The Edge of The Newness
Grandpa's spirit surely will soar.

Grandpa's greatest concern about death is leaving
Grandma. Grandpa has been taking care of Grandma every
since she was a young girl. Grandpa has witnessed great
emotional distress and heartache in families at the time of
death, caused by a lack of planning and lack of communi-
cation of information concerning funeral arrangements,
financial matters, and other vital information to the surviv-
ing spouse and children (many good businessmen are
guilty of this). Grandpa and Grandma have been preparing
for this transition for many years, and more especially the
last four years. Grandpa has prepared a "Red Folder" that
contains the following Memo to Grandma, and a step-by-

step guide to follow at the time of death. It gives the telephone number of the funeral director (preplanned including burial plot), pastor and others who will need to be contacted. This folder also includes a complete list of assets and the monthly income Grandma can expect to receive. It lists all insurance policies and procedures for collecting them, their location in the lock box, and any other pertinent information, such as the lock box number at the bank and where another copy of this information and both Grandpa and Grandma's wills are located. This information is updated several times each year, or as needed. A copy of the Memo follows:

MEMO TO MY DEAR WIFE

The following instructions and information are given to help you at the time of my death. They are listed in the order of their priority as I understand them. They are not to be considered as legally binding, but as guidelines that will help you. If it is to your advantage, feel free to do what is best for you at that particular time. <u>"TAKE ONE STEP AT A TIME."</u> At the time of my heart attack, you gave me a key chain and charm on which was inscribed these words, "One day at a time." Following this suggestion with God's help, you will find you are sufficient for anything that will happen to you in the future. I would recommend that you make no major changes for at least one year. This will allow you to make better decisions. You will have made your emotional adjustments, and your mind will function much better after the healing process. If you follow the six steps suggested in this "Red Folder" you should find that you can choose about any life style you want if you use your income wisely. Buy what you need, for you will have adequate income.

I submit this memo and information to you with all my love and prayers. It will help you if you use it as a guide.

I have loved you all these years and deeply appreciate all you have done for me and what you have enabled me to become. Without you, I would have accomplished nothing, and I would have become much less. I am grateful for your love and faithfulness. I have tried to be a good husband and father with God's help. At times I have failed. Please forgive me. May God bless and guide you until we are reunited in His Presence.

Love,

Your husband and friend (Grandpa)

Grandpa says, "Dying is a process over a period of time. Death is the Divine moment when I leave the old shell in which I have lived throughout my earthly journey. This is a Divine moment because God is in control of the experience of death, and he holds it in his good hands."

Grandpa believes that death is a very serious and sacred experience, but there are times when it is appropriate to laugh and smile. We should never suppress a normal need to laugh. It is not a sin to laugh and smile in the presence of death. Grandpa says, "I have witnessed deaths in which a moment of humor was provided by the dying person, I have found this to be a cherished moment of healing for a loved one or the family. We should never seek to produce laughter in a cheap way in this sacred hour, but we should also feel free to express normal emotional reactions, including laughter."

Grandpa knows that his long earthly journey will soon come to an end, and his feet will no longer be able to carry him any further. Grandpa knows his heart will cease to function and at a precise moment, death will come in God's good time. Grandpa doesn't like death, or want it to happen. He does not wish to leave Grandma (or have her leave him). Grandpa does not want to leave his children, grandchildren, or great-grandchildren. He has no desire to leave his many friends that he has made during his long journey. However, it is a realistic fact that his body is wearing out and one day he shall not be able to enjoy any of his family, and his earthly life will have no meaning and purpose. The divine moment will come to set him free from pain, limitations that have accumulated, and the worn out body will no longer be able to function. The divine moment of death will come as a friend. Grandpa does not worry about the details of how and when it shall happen for he is in the good hands of a God who is like Jesus.

Grandpa's imagination and mind have been influenced by reason, scripture, and by the life and teachings of Jesus for many years. Grandpa shares out of his imagination a picture of what he believes will happen at the moment of death as he leaves the old worn out body and steps over the edge of newness into the future. When a baby bird leaves its shell it bursts out into new life, discarding the broken shell. Grandpa sees this as a picture of what will happen to him. He will discard the old broken body with all its limitations, pain, and worn out parts. As Grandpa breathes his last earthly breath, he will no longer be tired. His aches and pains will be shed, Grandpa will burst into a new world that defies description in mere human terms. The first thing of which Grandpa is aware is a brilliant soft light. Grandpa SEES a pure and perfect light (All vision imperfections are gone). The light seems familiar. He quickly realizes that this is the Light of the World. It is Jesus!

Grandpa <u>HEARS</u> (Hearing impairments are gone), a voice so kind and gentle, with authority. It is a voice Grandpa has heard many times. . ."Come in son and enjoy the place I have prepared for you." He immediately knows it is the voice of Jesus. Grandpa hears the most beautiful music. Someone is singing a solo, "Worthy is the Lamb." Grandpa looks in the direction from which the sound is coming, and there is a smiling Kid Brother standing in the midst of a gigantic choir that is humming as he sings. He looks more closely, and seated at the console of a huge organ is Little Sister with a big smile on her face. She has a straight back with a new glorified body. The choir suddenly bursts forth singing, King of Kings! And Lord of Lords. King of Kings! And Lord of Lords! Hal-le-lu-jah! Hal-le-lu-jah! Hal-le-lu-jah! Hal-le-lu-jah! Grandpa hears the full chords, and enjoys this heavenly music. Grandpa's hearing is perfect. It is unbelievable! It transcends anything that words can describe. The endless corridors of heaven ring as everyone joins in the singing. Grandpa is amazed because the limitations on his hearing are gone, and he can sing even better than he could in his youth. Grandpa can hear the full chords as they vibrate through heaven. It is beyond comprehension. All Grandpa can think of are the words of Paul, "Eye has not seen, ear has not heard, neither has entered into the mind of man what God has prepared for those who love him."

Grandpa SEES mom and dad playing with little children. It is his brother and sister who died in infancy. They are really having fun, and Jesus himself takes the children up in his arms and blesses them. Teddy is lying at their feet wagging his tail! WOW! What a homecoming.!

Grandpa notices an endless line of large computer monitors. He was thinking about what a great time he could have with them. Saint Peter walks by, and Grandpa dares to ask him how you get permission to use the computers. Saint Peter says, "You don't have to ask anyone, just use them. You don't need to turn them on or off. All you have to do is look straight into the screen. You don't use any switches, keys, mouse or anything. Just think the question, look straight into the monitor and the answer will appear." Grandpa looked into a screen and thought "Are you on internet?" There was an immediate reply, "You don't need Internet. I am ETERNAL-NET. I am the source of all truth." Wow! How about that! Grandpa is overcome with joy. No limits on LEARNING! Now Grandpa understands what Paul meant when he wrote, "It is like this, when I was a child I spoke and thought and reasoned as a child does. But when I became a man, my thoughts grew far beyond those of my childhood, and now I have put away the childish things. In the same way, we can see and understand only a little about God now, as if we were looking at his reflection in a poor mirror; but someday we are to see him in his completeness, face to face. Now all that I know is hazy and blurred, but then <u>I will see everything clearly</u>, just as clearly as God sees into my heart right now." (Living Bible-paraphrased) Grandpa says, "Am I ever learning!

Grandpa <u>SMELLED</u> the most wonderful odor that ever entered his nostrils. It is fantastic! Grandpa discovered a table that reaches as far as the eye can see. The length of the table is endless, and it is loaded with beautiful fruits, vegetables of all color, exquisite flowers, meats of all kinds, breads galore, and much more (Grandpa keeps looking. Would you believe? Small chunks of ham in beans!) There are people of all races and colors who are gathered at the table joyfully celebrating the glorious God of all truth and grace. Grandpa's family is all there preparing to enjoy the feast. God is present everywhere at once. Grandpa is face to face with the God of love. He is speechless. God touched Grandpa's shoulder and says, "It's your time to express our gratitude." Grandpa stammered and said, "Thank you Heavenly Father for all these wonderful things, Amen! Please pass the ham and beans!"

God smiled, and the majestic and endless corridors of heaven reverberated with joyful laughter!

To order additional copies of **What Makes Grandpa Tick?**, complete the information below.

Ship to: (please print)

Name _____

Address _____

City, State, Zip _____

Day phone _____

_____ copies of *What Makes Grandpa Tick?*

@ $12.00 per copy $_____

Residents of IL add sales tax (.06)

$.72 per book $ _____

Total amount enclosed $ _____

Make checks payable to Marshall H. Ervin

Send to: **Books of Joy**
509 West Madison St., Rushville, IL 62681

- -

To order additional copies of **What Makes Grandpa Tick?**, complete the information below.

Ship to: (please print)

Name _____

Address _____

City, State, Zip _____

Day phone _____

_____ copies of *What Makes Grandpa Tick?*

@ $12.00 per copy $_____

Residents of IL add sales tax (.06)

$.72 per book $ _____

Total amount enclosed $ _____

Make checks payable to Marshall H. Ervin

Send to: **Books of Joy**
509 West Madison St., Rushville, IL 62681